Coriolis Effect

An Ed Lazenby Mystery

Charles Ray

Uhuru Press
North Potomac, MD

For information about this and other works of this author, contact the author at charlesray.author@yahoo.com.

Cover art and design by the author.

Author photo by Denise Ray-Wickersham

Printed in the United States of America.

ISBN: 0692661158
ISBN-13: 978-0692661154

DEDICATION

For all you amateur detectives out there.

ONE

Ed Lazenby hated being treated as a hero. He hated being called a hero. He hated it even more than he did the tufts of gray hair growing in his ears, that kept coming back no matter how many times he shaved them, and that stood out against his medium brown skin like pimples on prom night. As far as he was concerned, he was no hero. It was no fun at all having people following him around like he was some rock star.

Oh sure, he and his best friend, Ernesto Cardozo, had played a key role in rescuing their friend Violet Wertheim from the clutches of the handyman, Louis Palmer, and his confederate, Vincent Ghiaradelli, a local gangster wannabe, who had kidnapped her under the mistaken impression that she was a wealthy heiress. But, that had been pure luck, and he'd almost become a victim himself in the process.

He was just lucky. That didn't make him a hero. Dammit, he thought, I am no hero.

Despite his protestations, despite what he thought, his feelings weren't even given a second thought. And, he protested a lot. He told everyone within earshot that he was no hero.

None of that mattered, however, to the other residents of Potomac Valley Community, the slightly overpriced retirement community that Ed had called home for just over three years. It didn't help that Ernesto told the story to anyone who would listen, and in a community of cottages and condos of people on the far north side of 65, there was always a willing audience, so the story of their bravery, which Ernesto embellished with new 'facts' with each telling, spread around PVC, as they lovingly called their collection of small houses, cottages, and apartments, on a regular basis.

Ed pulled his jacket collar up around his ears against a sudden icy blast of arctic wind as he walked from his house to the community center near the main entrance. He was on the way to his usually Sunday brunch, only this time, with a dif-

room of the community center at 10:00 on Sunday morning, and watched the rest of the community while they ate their scrambled eggs, tuna salad, hashed brown potatoes, in-season fruit, and waffles, washed down with cup after cup of coffee—their combination breakfast and lunch. Ernesto, though, had gone to Norfolk, Virginia to visit cousins for New Year's Eve celebrations, and wasn't due back until late that evening. So, Ed was eating alone, which was fine with him. The only other PVC residents he had much contact with were the Wertheim sisters, Violet and Rose, and they too were visiting relatives somewhere in Idaho, or one of the other western states which, as far as Ed was concerned, might as well be on the far side of the Moon. He'd never had much love for the northwest, since its winters were as cold as the northeast, and the people he'd encountered during occasional trips to military bases in the region when he worked at the Pentagon hadn't been the friendliest. Places like Idaho and Utah, sparsely populated as they were, tended to breed the kind of people Ed had never found easy to get along with.

He shoved his hands deeper into the pockets of his tan North Face jacket, and again mentally congratulated himself for picking it up on sale the previous October at the Old Navy store on Rockville Pike. Temperatures had taken a steep dive in late November, buried themselves in December, and so far, on the fourth of January showed no signs of coming out of their hole and into a range that was comfortable to anything but a polar bear. His long legged stride took him past several couples walking bent forward against the wind, looking frail enough to blow away at any moment. When he got to the double glass doors of the main entrance, he stopped and held the door for one particularly frail looking couple, their faces bright red from the cold, who clung together as if afraid the wind *would* blow them away if they didn't.

"Thank you, Edward," the old woman said, looking up at Ed with watery blue eyes from which tears streamed. "How are you today?"

Ed struggled to remember their names, gave up, and smiled down at her. "I'm fine," he said. "A bit cold for my liking, though. How are you two?"

The man, about half an inch shorter

than the woman, with brown rather than blue eyes, frowned at Ed with razor thin lips. "How do you think we are, young fellow? We're freezing in this damn cold and the heat in our apartment's on the blink, so we're cold even when we're at home. We come here to eat the lousy food because it's the only warm place in the whole damn community. That's how we are, thank you."

The woman punched the man's arm and glared down her aquiline nose at him. "Simon, I'm sure Edward's not interested in your comments about the cold." She looked back up at Ed. "We're okay. Simon's right about the cold, though. It is a little bitter."

"I'll be glad when spring comes myself," Ed said, wishing the two would hurry through the door so he could get inside out of the cold himself.

Finally, they shuffled through, the old man still mumbling, and the woman still poking at his arm. Ed stepped inside and let the door whoosh shut behind him. He paused a moment to allow the circulation come back into his numb fingers and toes, and when he felt the first tinges of pain indicating that blood was flowing normally, he walked across the entrance lobby to the dining room.

Inside, the room was only sparsely populated, due, Ed surmised, to the cold weather. Just as well, he thought. It meant he didn't have to worry about having someone sitting at his table with him either gushing about his heroism, or interrogating him about the incident. He'd never been able to decide which he hated more. The adulation was embarrassing, but when people started asking him for details it became downright ghoulish, reminding him of people who slowed their cars when approaching an accident scene in hopes of catching a glimpse of blood and gore.

Due to budget cuts dictated by PVC's director, Dr. Roland Vickers, staff cuts had been made, so for weekend meals there was only one person on duty in the dining room, which meant residents had to get their own drinks. The drinks, coffee, tea, water, and a selection of juices and soft drinks in cans and bottles, were on a long table at the far end of the dining room near the door to the kitchen. This enabled the one staffer, this Sunday morning a skinny young woman with bright red hair and buck teeth named Norma, to replenish drinks between trips back and forth to the kitchen to keep the food tables filled. Norma darted in from the kitchen with a large rectangular container of hashed brown potato patties. She dumped them onto the tray under the infrared lamp warmer and quickly returned to the kitchen before anyone could talk to her. Ed could sympathize. His neighbors were a querulous, demanding lot at the best of times, and meal times were not the best of times.

He joined the line at the drink table, looking up at the swirling patterns in the plaster on the ceiling and hoping no one would want to talk as they shuffled forward to get drinks. His luck held; he got to the table, picked up a carafe of coffee and a glass of grapefruit juice, which he took to a table in the corner near the side window. He chose that location because, being near the window, it was a bit chilly, and most of the seniors avoided it.

After depositing his drinks he returned to the long table adjacent to the drink table, picked up a brown plastic tray from a stack at the end, and started loading up for brunch. He'd only had a bowl of cereal and a cup of coffee for breakfast when he'd awakened at his usual 6:00 am, so his stomach began to growl as soon as his nose came within range of the aroma of bacon and sausage in a large tray at the end of the table. He loaded a plate with both, and then stacked two hash brown patties next to the pile of meat. Scrambled eggs, pinto beans, fried tomatoes and four biscuits—on a second plate—completed his meal.

Back at his table, he sat with his back to the corner, facing the entrance door, hunched over his food and began eating. He had a . . . let's just call it a ritual . . . when it came to eating. It wasn't so elaborate that people noticed, although his friend Ernesto had, and often chided him about it, it was just an unvarying procedure he followed. He would take a small bite of everything on his plate, or plates, individually, chewing and enjoying the individual flavors, starting usually with the meat or meats and working his way clockwise around the plate. Once that was done, he'd then finish his meal no differently than anyone else, mixing and matching flavors and textures at random. It was just that he liked savoring the individual tastes first; had, in fact, since childhood.

Another habit he had, that also only Ernesto had ever noticed, was that of periodically scanning the dining room, paying particular attention to the entrance, while he ate. When his friend had asked him about it, he'd replied that he liked to know with whom he was dining. In truth, he wasn't sure why he did it. It was something he'd been doing for as long as he could remember. He just felt uncomfortable in a public place when he couldn't see who else was there, and who was coming and going.

He watched as he ate. A bit of bacon, and watched the door while chewing. Paid attention to spreading some jam from one of those little packets onto half a biscuit, and then watched the door as he shoved it into his mouth and chewed it.

During the first half of his meal, only a few people, all couples, came and went—mostly came, as everyone extended their meal as long as possible to stay in the warmth of the dining room, especially those nearest the door to the kitchen from which issued a steady stream of warm air. Ed would have liked sitting there, had in fact often done so in the past, but it would have meant enduring the comments and questions, so he endured the chilly draft by the window.

Just as he was lifting a fork of scrambled eggs to his mouth he glanced over at the door. A young by PVC standards couple were just coming through when they were roughly shoved aside by a short woman with stooped shoulders and ultra-wide hips wrapped in a gray shawl. Her face, red from the cold wind, was set in a frown, and she pushed between the surprised couple without looking back. The man muttered something that Ed couldn't make out, but the woman laid a hand on his arm and shook her head. The intruder continued to bull her way across the dining room toward the drink table. Ed chuckled and turned his attention back to his food. Such scenes weren't that common in PVC, but they did happen on occasion. He recognized the woman, but couldn't recall her name. All he remembered was that she was one of the elderly singles who happened, like him, to live in a small house rather than an apartment where most of the single residents lived. He'd seen her on occasion, but hadn't had a reason to speak to her, nor her to him.

Once the old woman and the disgruntled couple were well inside the dining room Ed turned his attention back to the two plates in front of him, now half empty, and started thinking about what he'd do for dessert. He was torn between the strawberry cheesecake and the gelatin with fruit cocktail. He was just about to throw in the towel and get both when he felt a presence behind him.

He turned in his chair, and there stood the old woman, a steaming cup of coffee in her hand, staring down at him.

"You mind if I sit with you?" she asked in a gravelly voice.

Of course, he did mind. He'd taken the table in the coldest corner of the dining room for the express purpose of dining alone.

"Uh, if you're sure you don't mind the draft," he said. "It can get pretty cold in this corner."

She sat in the chair across from him and put her cup on the table. "I don't mind the cold. I'm from Michigan. Winters up there make this seem like spring to me. What's good for brunch today?"

Ed didn't quite know how to respond to her. They'd never been introduced, but she was talking to him—at him—like they were old friends. To give himself time to reply appropriately, he took a long sip of coffee.

"Well, the bacon and hash browns are both nice," he said after putting his cup down. "The biscuits are a little heavy, but with enough jam they're not too bad."

"What about the eggs?"

"Just so-so," he replied.

"Guess I'll have that," she said, stand-ing. "Don't go away, I'll be right back. I need to talk to you."

He sat back in his chair and watched her walk away. She took her time at the food table, finally returning with a single plate with two slices of bacon, a hash brown patty, a biscuit, and a small lump of scrambled eggs. She put the plate on the table and took some time adjusting her napkin on her lap. Ignoring Ed, she forked a bit of egg in her mouth and took her time chewing it. Ed continued sipping at her coffee.

After she'd finished her second forkful of food, hash browns this time, she put the fork down and leaned forward, fixing Ed with a steely gaze.

"I like that," she said. "You're a pa-tient man, not given to jumping to con-clusions or fidgeting. That'll come in handy."

"Come in handy for what?"

"I need you to help me find my grand-son," she said. "The little bastard's been missing for a week."

TWO

"If your grandson's missing," Ed said. "You should really call the police."

She took a sip of coffee, made a face, and put the cup down.

"Can't do that, leastways, it wouldn't do any good. See, Levi, that's my grandson's name, Levi is twenty-two, so he's an adult, so the police, they'd just say he's got a right to be gone if he wants to be gone. They'd just tell me he's tired of hanging around an old lady, and that he's not missing at all. But, I know better. He's missing, and I need him found."

Ed considered that for a few seconds. It made sense, actually. He tended to agree with the police. If he had to live with a grandmother with this woman's personality, he'd probably hit the road, too. But, his parents had taught him to always be polite to everyone, regardless.

"How do you know he's not just off somewhere having fun? I mean, you said he's twenty-two. At that age, people, especially men, can do some strange things."

She shook her head.

"No, I know my grandson," she said. "The little bastard's shiftless, as worthless as a bucket of warm spit, but he'd never go off without telling me. Something's wrong, I just know it."

"Even so, what do you expect me to do about it? You don't even know me."

"But, I do know you. Leastways, I know *of* you. You're the one that rescued that Wertheim woman when she got herself kidnapped."

"Well, I don't know you, and I wouldn't even know where to start looking for your grandson."

"Oh, I'm sorry," she said, smiling. "Where on earth are my manners?" There was no humor in her smile, and she didn't sound as if she gave a damn whether she was being polite or not. "I'm Abigail Crumley. I live on Magnolia Street, just a couple streets over from where you live. My grandson, Levi, he's my youngest son's boy, so he's got the same last name as me."

"Okay, so now I know your name. I know your grandson's name. But, I'm not a cop or a private detective. I don't have the resources to find anyone. You really, really need to talk to the police if you honestly think your nephew's missing."

Her already wrinkled face wrinkled further and her thin, cracked lips pursed like she'd just bit into an especially sour lemon. "Weren't you listening? The police aren't gonna be interested in a case like this. Oh sure, they'd take the report and make all kinda sympathetic noises, but as soon as I walked out of the police station, they'd throw the forms in a folder and forget it. No, you're my only hope."

There was something about the way she avoided eye contact with him when she spoke, and seemed to be folding in on herself, that made Ed nervous. Something wasn't quite right, but he couldn't put his finger on it. He *did* know that there wasn't a thing he could do to help her. Sure, he'd found where Violet Wertheim was being held, but that had mostly been luck, and if Ernesto hadn't come along when he did, he would have wound up being kidnapped himself, or worse, he could have ended up with his head caved in. He'd thought it was annoying to be treated like a hero, but to have this woman thinking he was some kind of Sherlock Holmes or something was beyond ridiculous. And, sitting at the coldest table hadn't kept her away.

"It that's the case," he said. "I'm afraid you're out of luck. I wouldn't even know where to start looking for your grandson."

She ignored him and launched into her family history, starting with her son, Gerald, who had married too young to his high school sweetheart, Kandi, and she sneered when she explained how the girl misspelled her name by using a 'K" and an 'I' instead of 'C" and 'y'.. His bride had been part of the wrong crowd in school, the kids who cut school, smoked behind the bleachers, and did drugs, and she hadn't grown out of it. Abigail suspected she'd been using drugs during her pregnancy, which explained all of young Levi's problems. When they weren't somewhere high on drugs, her son and his wife worked for a construction company in Frederick, Maryland, so they'd left Levi with her almost from the day he was born, which was fortunate, because the winter when he was ten years old, the two of them had gotten stoned to the gills and fallen asleep with a space heater too near the curtains in the trailer they occupied. The curtains had caught fire and they never woke up. The incident had traumatized Levi at first, but his parents had been more like distant relatives, Abigail said, so eventually he got over it—or so she thought. He'd never been too communicative, she said, and kept mostly to himself. She was the only person he had any kind of relationship with, and he was all the family she had left.

Abigail, now 69, had been a resident of PVC for four years. Her grandson had lived there with her for the first year, but had moved out when he turned 19, which was also the year he'd finally graduated from high school.

Those last years, from the time he was 14, had been turbulent, she said. Young Levi had become moody and withdrawn, and she later discovered that he'd been experimenting with drugs, although he hadn't as far as she knew used the hard drugs that had led to the death of his parents.

Even after he moved out, though, he visited regularly, and always kept his Nana, as he called her, informed of his whereabouts, until, that is, the past two weeks. After a visit to her just after

Christmas, she hadn't heard from him. It was, she said, as if he'd just dropped off the face of the earth.

"So, you see," she said, summing up. "I just know something's wrong." Her thin lips quivered. "I don't know who else to turn to if you don't help me."

Ed felt hemmed in, trapped even. During the telling of her story, some of Abigail Crumley's harshness seemed to have peeled away, revealing an immensely lonely and worried woman. One part of him wanted to flee the table, while another desperately wanted to help her. Neither feeling pleased him. The part that didn't want to help her made him feel ashamed, but the part that wanted to help her made him feel put upon. Caught between a rock and a hard place, he felt himself slowly caving in, but felt obligated to put up at least token resistance.

"You don't understand, Ms. Crumley—"

"Please, call me Abigail, or Abby," she said.

"Okay, Abigail," he said. "I don't know how I can help you if the police can't."

"I didn't say they *couldn't*, I said I don't think they *will* help. There's a difference. I think you can do it . . . I know you can, and I'm willing to pay you for your help."

"Pay? As in money."

"Yes, of course. I'll give you five thousand dollars if you'll find my grandson."

Charles Ray

THREE

The mention of money had pushed Ed over to the side of helping. He wasn't sure if it was strictly legal for him to accept money for what he promised to do. After all, he wasn't official by any stretch of the imagination. On the other hand, Abigail Crumley had said she would pay him in cash. With only his government pension and the pittance he got each month from Social Security to live on, it wasn't like he couldn't use the extra buck here and there. And, as long as no one else knew about, he figured all was good. Okay, he thought, that's a rationalization. What he was really was curious. *Let's hope curiosity doesn't kill this cat.*

After he agreed to help her, she invited him to come to her house so she could give him a photo of her grandson, but he begged off, saying he was meeting his friend Ernesto, but he would stop by on Monday and get it. It being Sunday and all, he convinced her, there was nothing he could do anyway, so she agreed. He promised to call her before coming over, and left her in the dining room staring morosely into her second cup of coffee.

Back at his house on Wisteria Lane, he put a kettle of water on the stove to heat, and changed into chinos and a cashmere sweater. He then made a cup of chamomile tea and went into his living room where he spent the rest of the afternoon sipping tea and reading the *Washington Post*.

Ernesto was due back from his trip by 5:30, but Ed still hadn't heard from him by 5:45, so he made himself a tuna salad sandwich and washed it down with more tea. After cleaning the plate and cup, he went back to the living room and turned on his radio. He'd been sitting there for two hours listening to classical music on the local NPR station when the doorbell rang.

He opened the door to Ernesto standing there with a broad smile on his brown face.

"Ola, amigo," Ernesto said. "Ain't you gonna invite me in? It's colder than a witch's ass in Alaska out here."

Ed stepped aside to let his friend enter.

"I thought you were due back before six," Ed said, looking at his watch.

Ernesto looked at his Rolex and laughed. "My flight was delayed. I just got back, dumped my bags and came over for our Sunday evening libation. Anything interesting happened while I was gone?"

While Ernesto made himself comfortable by taking over three-fourths of the sofa, Ed took a bottle of Jim Beam bourbon from the cabinet across the room. He brought the bottle and two tumblers back and put them on the coffee table, and sat in the easy chair that sat catty-corner from the sofa.

"You want it mixed or neat?" he

asked.

"Just a couple cubes of ice. It was a long flight."

Ed got up and headed for the kitchen. "Okay, sounds good. I'll fill you in on things after I get some ice."

He came back with a Pyrex bowl full of ice cubes. After putting two cubes in each of the glasses, he then filled them to near the brim with the amber liquid and passed one to Ernesto.

"Here's to the good life," he said, raising his glass.

Ernesto raised his glass to acknowledge the toast and then tossed back a fourth of its contents in two large swallows.

"A-a-h, now that's what I've needed all day." He put his glass down and rubbed at the stubble on his round cheeks. "So, amigo, what's been going on?"

Ed took a sip of his bourbon and then put his glass down on the coffee table across from Ernesto's.

"Not much," he said. "Just the usual griping about the weather . . . oh, and I got hired by Abigail Crumley to find her grandson."

Ernesto's hand, just reaching for his glass, paused in midair.

"You what?"

"You heard me. Abigail Crumley wants to pay me five thousand dollars to find her missing grandson."

"Yeah, that's what I thought you said. Why the hell would you want to do anything for the Wicked Witch of PVC?"

"The what? I never heard that nickname before. In fact, until this morning at brunch, I didn't even know her name."

"Well, that's what the people who know her call her," Ernesto said. "Woman's as mean as a rattlesnake, and probably just as dangerous if you ask me."

"How do you know so much about her?"

"Hey, pal, I used to work for the Post Office, remember? Call it an occupational hazard. I know everybody in my neighborhood. I never spoke to her, but I know her neighbors, and that's what they call her. If you don't know her, how'd you get hired to find her grandson . . . I think his name's Levi by the way . . .

if he's missing, why didn't she just go to the cops?"

Ed explained how she'd approached him during brunch, and her explanation for why she didn't want to call the police. "The kid's twenty-two, so technically, unless she has some hard evidence, he's not really missing."

"That makes sense, but why would she want to pay five thousand bucks to find him? If you ask me, it sounds suspicious."

"Ha, that's just because you always see the worse in everyone, Ernie," Ed said. "She's just a lonely old woman, and the way she explained it, he's her only living relative. Maybe she's just lonely."

"Five thousand bucks! That's a lot of lonely. So, when do we get started?"

"What's this we stuff? She hired *me*, and I'm not sure I want to share the money with you."

Ernesto's lips turned down in a frown. "And, here I thought you and me were best buds. Did I say anything about you sharing the money? Did I?"

"Well, no, but if you're helping,

you'd be entitled to a share."

"Oh, Eduardo, *mi amigo*, you wound me to the core of my being. I don't need the money. Hell, my Post Office pension's probably a lot higher than what the Defense Department's paying you. I don't need the money. And, if you think I'm gonna let you go off and have adventures all by yourself, you got another think coming. Now, what's our next move?"

Ed sighed. He'd known that as soon as he told Ernesto about it, he'd want to be part of it. He also knew that his friend was right about the difference in their pensions. Not that it mattered. He would, of course, share the money. And, if he'd been pressed he would have admitted that he was happy to have Ernesto along.

"I told her I'd get in touch tomorrow and get more information about Levi, and see where it goes from there."

Ernesto lifted his glass. "Okay, then, the game's afoot."

Charles Ray

FOUR

They'd finished half the bottle of bourbon before Ernesto decided it was time to stagger across the street to his house and get some sleep. Ed stumbled off to his own bed immediately after his friend's large frame cleared his doorway.

The ncxt morning, they met in the dining room at 7:00 for breakfast. Ed was still fighting headache from the bourbon, a thump, thump that beat right behind his eyes making them water. Ernesto still hadn't shaved, and he had bags under his bloodshot eyes, but was otherwise his normal cheerful self.

Over a heaping breakfast of scrambled eggs, home fried potatoes, sausage, and waffles they sat together at the table near the window. Few residents were up so early, so they had the room mainly to themselves, except for three couples across the room near the door to the kitchen and the attendant, a heavyset black woman with black braids coiled on both sides of her head, serving coffee and juice and keeping the food tables stocked.

"What time you gonna call the witch?" Ernesto mumbled around a mouthful of potatoes.

"I thought I'd wait until after lunch." Ed put his fork down and rested his elbows on the table, steepling his hands and resting his chin on his fingertips. "I don't really think this is gonna go very far, so no rush."

"So, you don't think the kid's really missing?"

"I don't know, he might be," Ed replied. "The Witch, I mean, Abigail, seemed sincerely worried when she told me about it. On the other hand, the way you describe her, if I were a twenty-two year-old, I'd be putting some distance between me and her."

"Yeah, know what you mean.

Okay, I'm still in."

The attendant came over to their table. "Mr. Lazenby, Mr. Cardoza, there's a man in the lobby says he wants to talk to you. Can he come in?"

"What man?" Ed asked.

"He didn't say," the woman said. "He just said it was important. Is it okay if he comes in?"

Ed and Ernesto shared querying looks. Ernesto shrugged.

"Okay, let him come on in," Ed said.

She turned and left the dining room. A few seconds later she came back, followed by a medium height white man with close cropped brown hair, wearing a dark blue suit that looked like it came off the rack at J.C. Penny, and black wingtip shoes that were highly shined. His square jaw was dark with stubble and he had bags under his eyes.

"Looks like a fed," Ernesto said. Ed nodded his agreement. The man had that look Ed had seen often in the CID guys who worked in the Pentagon, though they tended to be less rumpled.

The woman pointed at their table and veered off toward the kitchen. The man approached their table. He reached into his jacket and pulled out a black leather case when he arrived, opening it to display gold shield with an eagle at the top, a blue tab with the word 'INSPECTOR' and the eagle symbol with US Mail beneath, surrounded by 'United States Postal Service' and nine stars.

"Gentlemen, I'm Inspector Joshua Williams with the U.S. Postal Inspection Service," he said. "You are Edward Lazenby and Ernesto Cardoza?"

"Pleased to meet you, inspector," Ed said. He pointed to the empty chair at his left. "Won't you have a seat?"

Williams turned the chair around and straddled it. He looked across at Ernesto and then turned his attention to Ed, but remained silent.

"The strong silent type," Ernesto said.

"What can we do for you, inspector?" Ed asked.

"Are you gentlemen acquainted

with a Ms. Abigail Crumley?" Williams asked.

Ed and Ernesto shared another look.

"I met Ms. Crumley for the first time yesterday," Ed said.

"I know her name, but have never personally met her," Ernesto said.

"Why do you want to know?" Ed asked.

"I'm sorry I'm not at liberty to divulge that information, Mr. Lazenby. You say you met her yesterday? What did you talk about?"

Ed felt a nagging tickle at the base of his skull. He wasn't fond of getting what seemed like the third degree. The man was asking personal questions, and he hadn't told Ed why he wanted—or needed—to know. He didn't like withholding information from a law enforcement official, especially a federal official, but ever since September 11, 2001 and the subsequent passage of the Patriot Act, many federal agencies had been overreaching in their so-called war on terrorism. Not, he thought, that anyone could be suspecting Abigail Crumley of being a terrorist—a terror, yes, but not a terrorist. A little voice in his head told him that some things should remain private. After all, her missing grandson wasn't the federal government's business.

"We just talked about the weather," he said. "Well, mostly she talked. Complained about the cold the whole time she sat here. Right here at this very table, in fact."

"She didn't talk about any business ventures she or her family might be involved in?"

"No," Ed said. "Like I said, she only talked about the weather."

"I see. Do you know anything about Ms. Crumley's family?"

"No, as far as I know she doesn't have anyone. She's a widow." Ed didn't look at Ernesto when he spoke, hoping his friend wouldn't say anything to expose his lie. He need not have worried. Ernesto was on his 'A' game.

"Yeah," Ernesto said. "Like I said, I never met her, but from the people I've talked to that know her, she's got no next of kin that anybody knows."

Ed breathed a small sigh of relief.

"Something wrong, Mr. Lazenby?" Williams asked.

"No, I just have a touch of gas. You know how it is with us senior citizens; our stomachs are always acting up."

"You think his breathing's bad," Ernesto chimed in. "You oughta be around when he eats beans. If the UN ever finds out, they're gonna accuse him of chemical warfare and lock him away in a bunker somewhere."

Williams regarded them through narrowed eyes, but said nothing. He cleared his throat. "Oh, sorry about that. I hope it clears up soon," he said. He stood. He removed a card from his pocket and put it on the table. "Thank you gentlemen for your time. I'm sorry to have interrupted your meal. If you should think of anything about Ms. Crumley that might be useful, please give me a call."

"It would help if we knew what this was all about," Ed said. "How are we to know what might be helpful if we don't know what you're investigating?"

"I'm sorry, but I'm just not at liberty at the moment to share that information. Good day, gentlemen." Without waiting for them to respond, he turned and walked away.

"Now, that was passing strange," Ernesto said.

"Indeed it was. What do you make of it?"

"Well, for one thing, it's probably not terrorism. The Postal Inspection Service usually investigates cases of mail fraud or theft."

"I remember reading about them being involved in the investigation of the anthrax letters back several years ago. Wasn't that domestic terrorism?" Ed said.

"Yeah, they did, and if it'd been after 9/11 they would have called it domestic terrorism. The reason they got involved was because the letters went through the mail. They worked with the FBI. In fact, it was the postal inspectors who actually broke the case. Say, you don't think Abigail's some kind of mail order terrorist, do you?"

"Hell no. She's an old curmudgeon, but terrorism? No way. By the way, thanks for backing me on her not having any relatives. I hate holding information back from a federal cop, but until we know more about what's going on, I think it's best that our friend Williams not know about Levi."

"No problem, buddy. I don't have a problem not telling. Hell, he held information back from us, so the way I figure it, we're just taking a page from his playbook. So, what do we do now?"

Ed pulled his cell phone from his pocket.

"We go see Abigail."

Charles Ray

FIVE

Ed called the switchboard, and after five minutes of argument got Abigail Crumley's number. He called her and arranged to see her at her house at 11:30.

Donning their jackets, Ed and Ernesto went out to the main parking lot. Ed wanted to check and see if Postal Inspector Williams might still be lurking around. Lurking was the term Ed's mind came up with, for it fit the way the man had conducted himself. The nerve, he thought, using the tired cliché, 'I'm not at liberty to divulge that.' The more he thought about it, the more he felt not sharing information with Williams had been a good idea. After walking in a zig zag pattern through the whole lot and not spotting an official looking vehicle with US Government plates, they set out to Abigail Crumley's house.

She lived in a house that was similar to Ed's, but it was set back a bit more from the street than his, thus giving it a bigger front lawn. Actually, except for the larger lawn, and with green trim rather than the plain white trim Ed had, it was identical. The builders hadn't shown a lot of creativity. He was pleased at least, knowing that this meant a tiny, postage-stamp-sized backyard which would be totally unusable for cookouts, something he and Ernesto alternated doing at least twice a month during the warmer months. Of course, he reckoned as he and Ernesto strode up the walkway toward her front door, Abigail Crumley didn't seem like the entertaining type, so it hardly mattered. In fact, it might be why she chose the place. She didn't seem to be much of a front yard place either, if the brown, patchy appearance of her lawn was any indicator. Ed prided himself on maintaining a healthy, lush front lawn, and through hiring a lawn service to come in once a month, so did Ernesto. Abigail's lawn, other than looking like it was cut monthly to comply with community grass length rules, appeared to be as neglected as the highways and bridges across the country; it looked good when it was first constructed, but was never maintained.

Ed pressed the brass button beside the door. Even her doorbell had a sour personality. The harsh buzzing sound reminded Ed of the electronic locks on secure doors in the Pentagon, the alarms that sounded like a swarm of angry wasps. After three buzzes, Abigail came to the door.

As Ed expected, she met them with a sour look on her narrow face; a look like she'd been sucking on unripe limes.

When she saw who it was, the frown straightened out. Not into a smile, just a neutral expression as if she was undecided whether to be happy, sad, angry or disappointed.

"Oh, it's you," she said. "Come on in."

She stepped aside to let them enter.

The living room reflected her personality even more than the doorbell did. All harsh angles and austere colors, the room looked more like the waiting room of a doctor's office—maybe a proctologist or a dentist—than it did a place where someone normal lived. The furniture was all angles and straight lines; mostly silver colored metallic chairs and small tables, with a couple of upholstered chairs in dull gray fabric, but even they had angular armrests and straight backs. It was arranged in precisely aligned settings with just enough room between pieces for one person to navigate without banging a shin. The walls were wallboard covered with slightly textured plaster, and were a bluish gray, which caused some of the furniture to appear from a distance to be one-dimensional. Abigail matched the furniture and walls. Her complexion was grayish, with thin eyebrows that looked as if they'd been painted on with a dark gray pencil, iron gray hair pulled severely back and ending in a small bun, and she wore a gray one-piece dress with a gray pixie collar buttoned tight against her angular neck.

"We came to get the information about your grandson," Ed said, figuring her for the type not given to small talk.

"Have a seat and I'll get his photograph so you'll know what he looks like," she said. She turned and exited through a door opposite the entrance without offering them a seat.

"Real friendly type," Ernesto said.

"I figured she'd be dressed in black," Ed said. "Given her nickname, but I see at home she's more into gray."

"Maybe we oughta start calling her the Gray Witch."

"Hush," Ed whispered. "She might hear you."

Ernesto blushed. "Sorry."

Abigail returned to the living room carrying a photograph clutched to her flat chest.

"Have a seat," she said.

Ed and Ernesto sat on a gray

couch. The cushions were so thin Ed could feel the hardness of the wooden frame pressing against his buttocks.

"May I see the picture?" he asked.

She sat on a metal chair across from them and handed the photo across the table.

"That was taken last year," she said. "His hair's a little longer now I think, but otherwise that's what he looks like."

Ed took the photo and held it so Ernesto could look at it with him. It was a color photo of a thin young man with the same grayish complexion as his grandmother, but with close-cropped brown hair. He wore a Washington Redskin's sweatshirt and faded jeans, and was standing beside a gray van. The picture appeared to have been taken in front of Abigail's house during the fall if the brown patches that Ed could see on the lawn were any indication.

"What does your grandson do for a living?" he asked.

"He does deliveries."

"What company does he work

for?"

She looked down at her hands folded in her lap. "He doesn't work for any company," she said. "He's self-employed."

Ed leaned forward, his brown forehead creased. "I don't understand. What kind of deliveries does he do?"

She fiddled with her bony fingers, still studying her hands. "There's this mail place down on Georgia Avenue, it's called Mail Box or something like that. When people get a lot of packages and they don't want to go down and pick them up themselves, they hire Levi to go down and get them and deliver them to their homes."

Ed looked at Ernesto who just made a noncommittal grimace.

"Don't look at me," Ernesto said. "I never heard of that kind of service either. But, it doesn't surprise me. You got all kinds of places and people competing with the Post Office these days, so I guess it was just a matter of time until somebody started replacing postal carriers."

"Do you have the address of this

. . . Mail Box?" Ed asked Abigail.

"No, but if you turn left when you leave the front gate, you can't miss it," she said. "It's about two or three miles down Georgia Avenue on the left, or maybe on the right. I can't rightly recall, but you can't miss it."

"What about Levi's friends? Can you give me their names?"

Now, she looked at him, frowning. "Why do you need to know all this?"

"If you want me to find him, I have to know where to start looking. His place of work and friends he might hang out with are the best places to start. For instance, does he have a girlfriend?"

She screwed her face up in concentration. "Far as I know he doesn't have a girlfriend, and he's never mentioned any friends to me. Levi's not exactly the social type. He pretty much stays to himself."

"You said he moved out; do you know where he lives?"

She shook her head. "No, he never told me. He stays . . . stayed here with me some weekends. I don't know where he went when he didn't stay here."

Ed was starting to feel frustrated. How, he thought, was he supposed to find a missing person with so little to go on? And, furthermore, how could someone supposedly so interested in finding her only relative be so ignorant of them?

"Do you mind if I take a look at his room?"

Her eyebrows shot upwards. "His room . . . why do you need to see his room?"

"It might give me an idea of where to start looking for him."

She looked as if she was about to say no, but then, her shoulders sagged.

"Okay," she said. "When he stays here, he sleeps in the guest bedroom, well, it was really *his* bedroom, but now he's gone, I'll use it as a guest room . . . unless he comes back—I mean, when he comes back. Come on, I'll show you. I have to warn you, though, it's probably messy. I refuse to clean it for him, and that boy's never learned to pick up after himself."

She stood and started toward

the door at the right side of the living room. It led into a short hallway with three doors. The first on the right was open, which she walked past. Ed took a quick look through the open door as they passed. A big four poster bed with a faded powder blue blanket, a three drawer nightstand with an alarm clock and a small lamp, and a straight back chair, neatly arranged. A pair of wooly slippers sat on the gray carpet under the middle of the bed. What he could see of the walls had the same institutional look as the living room. This, he figured, had to be Abigail's bedroom. It reflected her austere, colorless personality perfectly. The first door on the left, she also passed. He assumed that was the guest bathroom. She stopped at the last door on the left, opened it and stepped aside for Ed and Ernesto to enter.

Ed stopped a few steps into the room and looked around. Behind him he heard Ernesto's intake of breath. Except for the gray carpet and colorless wallpaper, it was the opposite of the almost military neatness of Abigail's bedroom, or the living room.

A double bed in the center of the far wall was covered by a rumpled green blanket. Two pillows, one without a pillow case, lay haphazardly propped against the headboard. A scuffed pair of brown boots sat forlornly in the corner, one of them with a dirty pair of boxer shorts draped over the top. There were water rings on the scarred night table, and the alarm clock lay face down on the table's surface. Several empty cardboard boxes, the size used for packing books and small items, were scattered about the floor. Against the wall opposite the foot of the bed was a four-drawer dresser, as scuffed and scarred as the night stand. On its top were several empty 8 by 10 brown envelopes and some white legal sized envelopes. There were no pictures on the wall. In fact, Ed realized as he looked around the room, there were no pictures in the living room.

To add to the disconnect between this room and the rest of the house, which seemed as sterile and unoccupied as a stage set, there was a slight wet dog odor in the air in the room. Unlike his grandmother, Levi Crumley was a slob.

But, there was nothing in plain sight in the room that gave a hint of where he might be. Ed wanted to take a look in the closet or the drawers of the dresser or night stand, but one look at the disapproving look on Abigail's face told him that that might be a bridge too far. She stood in the door with her arms folded across her chest, tapping her left foot on the carpet. He and Ernesto had clearly overstayed their welcome.

"Okay," he said. "I don't think there's anything helpful here, so I guess we'll have to start with the place where he picks up packages. I have to tell you, though, we don't have a lot to go on. I can't promise you we'll be able to find him."

Her eyebrows did the upward arch again. "We, what do you mean we? I only promised to pay you," she said.

"Don't worry about me," Ernesto said. "I'm just along for the ride. Ed needs a wheel man so he can do the brain work. Won't cost you extra at all."

She frowned, causing her eyebrows to bunch toward the bridge of her nose. Then, she shrugged. "Okay, I guess that's okay. You need anything else?"

"No, we'll get started looking right away," Ed said. "I'll let you know if we find anything."

Wordlessly, they followed her back to the living room and to the exit. She opened the door for them, and after they were outside, closed it. Ed heard the snick of the lock closing.

When they were back at the street Ernesto turned to him.

"That is one strange old broad," he said.

"That, my friend, is the understatement of the century," Ed said. "You ready to do some snooping?"

Ernesto shrugged. "It's too cold to play golf, and too early in the day to drink, so why not."

Charles Ray

SIX

They took Ed's 1999 silver Toyota 4-Runner. Ernesto had argued for his fire engine red 2010 Chevy Silverado, but Ed hated riding in pickups, especially red ones with a cartoon picture of a dog on a short leash tied to a stake on each door with the slogan, 'That'll teach you to mess with the mailman.' Besides, he argued, since they were going to be out anyway, they could stop at the Giant Food Store on Georgia Avenue and stock up on foodstuffs and he'd rather not carry groceries in the back of the pickup.

Abigail had been wrong. The Mail Box store was *four* miles away, in a strip mall tucked between a

Dairy Queen and a Radio Shack,
which also, Ed noticed with delight,
contained a Giant Food grocery
store. It was on the west side of
Georgia Avenue, which was the right
side from PVC. An electronic contact
in the door frame, activated when
they pushed the door open, sounded
the opening notes of *fur Elise*. A six-
foot-three, emaciated looking, pimply faced blond with a horrendous
overbite stood behind the counter.
His hair was filled with dandruff
flakes, and looked like it hadn't been
washed in forever. Behind him and
off to the left was a bank of medium-
sized mail boxes, the kind with bur-
nished brass doors just like in the
real Post Offices, and to the left of
that was a simple wooden door with
a sign that said, 'Employees Only.'

"Can I help you, gentlemen?" he
asked as Ed and Ernesto approached the counter.

Ed pulled Levi Crumley's photo
from his inside jacket pocket and
laid it on the counter.

"You know this man?" he asked.

Pimply face looked down at the
picture with about as much interest
as a vegan in a deli, then back at

Ed.

"Who wants to know?"

Ernesto made a growling noise deep in his throat and pushed forward, putting his beefy hands palm down on the counter and leaned in until his face was six inches from the clerk. Before he could say anything, Ed put a restraining arm across his chest.

"We're friends of his grandma. We live in the retirement community up on Georgia Avenue, Potomac Valley Community," Ed said.

Pimply face picked at a pimple on his left cheek and looked at the photo on the counter with the same expression one would use for dog poop on the bottom of one's shoe. Then, he looked back up at Ed, still picking at the pimple.

"So, what's that to me, pops?"

Ernesto made another growling sound that was higher up in his throat this time, and before Ed could stop him, he reached across the counter, grabbed the collar of the boy's blue jacket, and hauled him across the counter until his feet were sticking out behind and banging against the shelves behind the counter, and his stomach was creased by the corner of the counter.

"Umph!" Pimply face said. "Urgh!"

Ernesto held on to the collar with his left hand, while clenching his right into a ham-sized fist and bringing it back alongside his face.

"Here's what it is to you, punk," he said. "I used to work for the Post Office, and I don't much like people who put my old friends out of work, which is what places like this do. I also don't like smart mouth assholes who give my friend grief when he asks a simple question." He tightened his grip on the collar, causing Pimply face's cheeks to puff out and turn red. "And, I'm sure you know where the phrase 'going postal' comes from, right? Well, right now, I'm just about to go postal on your skinny white ass . . . comprende?"

The kid was grabbing at Ernesto's hand while trying to balance on the counter, and breathe at the same time. His face was turning redder and spittle was dripping out the sides of his mouth and sliding slowly down his gaunt cheeks. His eyes were wide. He twisted his head around to look pleadingly at Ed.

"Hey, dude, m-make him stop. He's choking me."

Ed shrugged. "I'm sorry, but you upset him. I can do nothing with him when he's upset, I'm afraid."

The kid's eyes swiveled to look up at a snarling Ernesto.

"Okay, okay, dude . . . p-please, don't hurt me. What do you want?"

"I want you to answer my friend's questions," Ernesto said. "And, no more bullshit or attitude out of you, or next time I'll squeeze harder."

"Y-yeah, okay, whatever you want. Uh, what was the question again?"

Ed stabbed the photo with his forefinger.

"Do you know this man?"

Ernesto still held the kid across the counter.

"Uh, yeah, that's Levi Crumley," Pimply face said.

"Does he work here?"

The kid's prominent Adam's apple bobbed up and down as he

pulled against Ernesto's hold on his collar. Ernesto made a growling sound at him.

"Yeah, uh, no," he said. "I mean, he don't actually *work* here. He ain't an employee of The Mail Box or nothing like that. He just like picks up bulk deliveries for customers who don't want to come and do it themselves. He got like this list of regular clients, I think, that he picks up for."

"Does he have access to their mail boxes?" Ernesto asked.

"Naw, man, he just like has access to his own box. We keep bulk deliveries in a room in the back, and he picks 'em up about once a week."

"How do you know which ones he's allowed to pick up?" Ed asked

"He got this list, see, and we got like signed releases from the customers."

"Show us the list," Ernesto said.

"Uh-uh, man," Pimply face said. "I can't do that unless you got like a warrant or something. That's private information. I'd get fired if I let you see it."

Ed looked at Ernesto. "Afraid he's got us there, amigo," Ernesto said.

"Can you at least tell us how many people he picks up for?" Ed asked.

Pimply face screwed his face up in concentration. "Uh, yeah, I guess that don't break no rules. He's got like four clients . . . I think."

"And, he picks up for them every week?"

"Yeah, man, every week . . . except, he ain't been in for over a week."

"Is there anything here for him to pick up today?" Ernesto asked.

"Sorry, man, but that's private information, too. Why you old dudes like asking all these questions about Levi?"

Ernesto growled at him one more time and then released his hold on his collar, causing him to slide off the counter. He rubbed at his throat and gulped.

"Sorry, kid," Ernesto said. "That's private information. If I told you, I'd have to kill you."

Pimply face's eyes cut from side to side, looking fearful when they looked at Ernesto, and pleading when they were on Ed.

"He's k-kidding, right," he said to Ed. "He won't really like k-kill me, will he?"

"You never know," Ed said. "He is a retired postman."

They left him standing there goggling wide-eyed.

SEVEN

The Giant Food Store was about a hundred yards past The Mail Box, so Ed and Ernesto left the 4-Runner parked where it was and walked over to do their shopping. After an hour of stocking up on items for their respective pantries, they shoved two shopping carts full of their purchases back to Ed's vehicle.

As they approached, they saw a mountain of a man leaning against the left front wheel well. He was nearly seven feet tall, with shoulders so wide and bulging with muscle they strained against the dark blue windbreaker he wore. His skin was dark, so dark the shadows on his face looked blue, and he had tiny, close set eyes that stared indifferently at them His hairless head glistened in the afternoon light. His thick lips were set in a straight line.

They slowed their approach, studying him. He didn't appear to be menacing, other than his size, which was menace enough, just stared idly at them.

"This car belong to one of you gentlemen?" he asked as they swerved toward the rear. His high pitched voice sounded out of character coming from one so huge.

"Yes, it's mine," Ed said. "Can we help you?"

"Naw, but the boss wants a word with you."

Ernesto stepped in front of Ed. "Who is this boss, and why does he want to talk to us?"

The big man blinked his piggy eyes at Ernesto as if puzzled at the question, or perhaps that anyone would *dare* question him. "The boss is Mr. Bosworth," he said finally. "And, it's up to him to tell you what he wants to talk about. I'm just here to escort you to him."

Ed could see Ernesto stiffening his shoulders. Not a good sign. That indicated he was ready to get stubborn and start a verbal battle. Unfortunately, the big man leaning casually against the vehicle didn't look the type who fought with words. Ed knew a little martial arts, and Ernesto was a pretty good barroom brawler, but the big man looked like he could take the two of them without ever moving from his place against the vehicle or working up a sweat. On top of it all, it had sounded more like a command than an invitation.

"Where is Mr. Bosworth?" Ed asked.

The big man pointed to the second row of cars behind the 4-Runner. Ed didn't need him to indicate which car; among the SUVs, vans, and rusty pickups in the parking lot the black Mercedes limo stood out like the 'Hollywood' sign in Los Angeles. The windows were tinted, so he couldn't see inside.

"Well," he said. "Let us put our groceries away, and lead on."

Ernesto frowned at him, but he only shrugged and stood there like a huge statue carved from ebony. After they'd put their purchases into the cargo area and relocked the vehicle, they fell in behind the behemoth who led them to the limo. When they arrived, he opened the rear door and stepped aside.

"Inside," he said. "The boss don't like letting cold air in."

Again, Ed shrugged. He stepped into the warm interior of the car, followed reluctantly by Ernesto who shot a glare over his shoulder at the big man. The door slammed shut as soon as Ernesto's backside cleared it. They found themselves in one of those luxury cars with two sets of rear seats, arranged facing each other. Between the rear-facing seats was a leather covered arm rest with depressions for drink containers. There were two glasses containing clear liquid in the depressions. A man sat on the forward-facing seat, in the center, making it clear that they were to sit facing him. He had milk-chocolate colored skin—more milk than chocolate—thin lips topped with a thin mustache, carefully sculpted eyebrows over almond-shaped, amber-colored eyes, and jet black hair slicked down and combed straight back on his oval skull. That and his slick looking gray suit with lapels a bit wider than the current fashion made him look like an entertainer from the 1950s jazz and do-wop era, when black performers pomaded their hair rather than let it grow naturally as was the practice during the Civil Rights era and afterwards. He held a crystal glass in a slender hand with long fingers whose nails shone like they'd been painted with some transparent substance. His almond eyes were unblinking as he watched them settle themselves into the cushiony leather seats. Ed felt like he was being eyed by a large reptile, sizing him up as a potential meal.

"So, you're Mr. Bosworth," Ed said after they were settled. "Why'd you want to talk to us?"

Bosworth smiled; an open-mouth smile that showed off brilliant white, even teeth. "Right down to business," he said with a faint trace of the Deep South in his accent. "I like that. So, business it is. I understand you two are trying to find Levi Crumley."

Ed noted that it was a statement, not a question. He wondered how this man knew what they were up to. The clerk at The Mail Box must have made a phone call after they left.

"Yes, as a matter of fact we are," he said.

"You mind me asking *why* you're looking for him?"

His first instinct was to tell this inquisitive stranger that it was none of his damn business. But, they were at a disadvantage. Trapped inside a car with a man who looked like central casting's idea of a black gangster, with a bodyguard outside bit enough to wipe the parking lot with them, the odds weren't in their favor. He decided that discretion was in order.

"No, I don't mind at all. His grandmother's worried about him. She asked us to find him. Why are you interested in why we're looking for him?"

Bosworth took a slow sip from his glass. "How do you gentlemen like your drinks? It's mineral water that I have flown in from Norway. Supposed to be . . . what that's term they use . . . regenerative, yeah that's what it is, regenerative."

Ed locked gazes with him. "You didn't answer my question, sir. Why are you interested in why we're looking for Levi Crumley:"

Bosworth waggled a long finger like a teacher admonishing a naughty student.

"Now, now, Mr. Lazenby, that's nothing for you to worry about. It's just a business matter. Why'd Levi's grandma ask you to find him; you some kinda expert on findin' people?"

"Not really," Ed said. "I got lucky when a neighbor was kidnapped. Now, people think I'm some kind of Sherlock Holmes, but I'm not. I'm just helping a neighbor."

Bosworth laughed. "Well, well, a modest man who don't like blowing his own horn. I like that. I like you Lazenby. Tell you what I'm gonna do. You keep looking for Levi, and when you find him, you give me a call." He took an engraved name card from his jacket pocket and handed it to Ed.

"Why would I want to do that?"

"Because I'm a nice guy, and

you're a nice guy." Bosworth laughed again. "Plus, I'll pay you ten thousand bucks for that one phone call."

Ed's mouth dropped open. Ernesto made a loud gulping sound.

"That's a lot of money," Ed said.

"Depends on your point of view," Bosworth said, waving dismissively. "I need very much to get in touch with young Mister Crumley, and as you can see from this car, I'm not without monetary resources. Hell, ten grand's not all that much."

"In other words, ten thousand's just chump change to you," Ernesto said.

"Colorfully put, Mr. Cardoza, but accurate I suppose. Do we have a deal?"

"Okay," Ed said, putting Bosworth's card in his jacket pocket. "Yes, if we find Levi, we'll give you a call."

"Good decision, I'll be waiting for your call."

As if a switch had been turned off, Bosworth was no longer paying them any attention. Ed poked Ernesto's shoulder to indicate he should get out of the limo. When they were back at Ed's 4-Runner, Ernesto looked at him across the roof.

"That guy's some kind of gangster, right?"

"What gave him away, the fancy car or the gorilla he sent to fetch us?"

"And, he wants to find Levi Crumley?"

"Yes."

"You think it's a good idea to turn the kid over to a gangster?"

"Not really."

"So, you're not gonna call Bosworth when we find him?"

"Now, why on earth would I want to do that?"

Charles Ray

EIGHT

Back at PVC, Ed stopped first at Ernesto's to drop him and his groceries off, and then he drove across the street and unloaded his own. He was just putting the last item away when his phone rang. He had to search for it among the messy jumble of paper groccry bags on the kitchen counter, but finally found it on the sixth ring.

"Hello," he said.

"Is this Edward Lazenby?" asked a male voice that Ed didn't recognize.

"Yes, who is this?"

"This is Inspector Joshua Williams. We spoke this morning, remember?"

"Inspector, what can I do for you?"

"I'd like to speak again with you and your friend. When's a good time?"

"I wasn't planning anything for the rest of the day," Ed said.

He gave Williams directions to his house, pressed the End Call button and immediately called Ernesto and informed him. Ernesto promised to come right over, and was ringing his doorbell ten minutes later.

"Come on in," Ed yelled from the kitchen door. "The door's not locked."

He was chopping lettuce when Ernesto entered the kitchen.

"Did Williams say why he wanted to talk to us?"

"No." Chop, chop. "Just said he wanted to see us." Chop, chop.

He used the side of the knife blade to scoop the lettuce into the sink. He turned on the cold water and briskly washed the lettuce.

"I wonder what he has on his mind," Ernesto said.

Ed took the lettuce out of the sink and dumped it into a medium sized bowl. He then dumped a pile of walnuts from a can onto the chopping board and began chopping them into tiny pieces.

"Wondering about something like that's a complete waste of time," Ed said. "Why don't you make yourself useful by brewing a pot of coffee."

While Ernesto fussed with the coffee maker, Ed tossed the chopped walnuts in with the lettuce and took a small apple from the refrigerator's crisper drawer. He washed, peeled, and chopped the fruit and added that to the bowl, stirring the ingredients with a fork until they were well mixed.

"What's this for?" Ernesto asked.

"I thought I'd have tuna sandwiches and salad tonight for supper, you want to join me?"

Ernesto made a face. "Nah, I think I'll just nuke a pizza and pop the tab on a can of beer. What you're making sounds too much like the food my food eats. I'll wait and get my vegetables already digested thank you."

Ed smiled at his friend and shook his head. "You know, if you don't start eating a healthier diet, you're gonna have real problems when you get old."

This was a standing joke between them. Ed on occasion switched from large helpings of meat and carbs at meals to healthier salads and sea-food or chicken, to give his arteries a chance to clear he'd always say, while Ernesto steadfastly refused to give up fried foods, red meat, eggs, or any of the other foodstuffs that were considered deadly. His re-sponse was always, "We're all gonna die someday of something. It might as well be something we were enjoy-ing when it killed us."

Ed put the finishing touches on the salad, which consisted of two tablespoons of non-fat mayonnaise mixed in well, then he covered the bowl with a square of plastic wrap and put it in the fridge. He decided to wait until just before supper to open a can of tuna and whip up a quick tuna salad.

Just as the coffee maker's bell signaled that the coffee was ready, the doorbell rang.

Ed and Ernesto walked into the living room. Ed checked through the narrow window next to the door.

"It's Williams," he said as he opened the door.

The postal inspector walked in. Once inside the room, he slid his blue North Face fleece collar jacket off, revealing dark brown cotton pants and a black, white and red plaid shirt. His pants topped a pair of black hiking boots. His hair needed brushing or combing, he had stubble on his cheeks, and there were bags under his eyes. He wasn't looking like a stereotypical federal agent, Ed thought, he looked more like an undercover local cop who'd just come from a night-long stakeout, or a homeless man who hadn't quite worn his wardrobe out. Ed motioned Williams to the sofa, but he took the chair opposite it instead, leaving Ed and Ernesto to sit side by side on the sofa like two truant students in the vice principal's office.

"Inspector Williams," he said. "To what do we owe the pleasure of this visit?"

Williams kept a passive face, but his eyes blazed as he looked from Ed to Ernesto.

"You two have been quite naughty," he said. "First, you lied to me about your relationship with Abigail Crumley."

"What makes you say that?" Ed asked.

"You went to see her right after I talked to you. That's not the actions of someone who barely knows a person."

Ed's brows went up a tiny fraction. Out of the corner of his eye he could see that Ernesto's mouth was hanging open. They'd checked the parking lot closely and had been sure there were no official vehicles there. But, he thought as he took in Williams' non-official looking dress, he might have been in an unofficial vehicle, conducting under cover surveillance or something.

"How do you know that?" Ernesto asked.

A tiny twinge of Williams' lips almost turned into a smile.

"I have my sources," he said. "We'll get to why you lied to me in a minute, though. There's something even more important to discuss. What were the two of you doing at The Mail Box, and why were you talking to Belmont Bosworth?"

Now, Ed didn't try to hide his surprise. The only way Williams could know that was he had *them* under surveillance.

"Have you been following us?" he asked.

Williams blinked at him. "No, I have not been following you," he said.

Ed sensed there was more the man hadn't said.

"Then, how is it that you know so much about where we've been or who we've been talking to?"

Williams rubbed at the stubble on his cheek. His brows crinkled. "Let's just say that I have it on good authority and leave it at that. You know, I could arrest you for interfering in a federal investigation. for lying to me about your relationship with Abigail Crumley. Consider yourselves lucky that I don't."

Ed held up a finger. "First of all, *Inspector Williams* , I didn't lie to you about that, nor did Ernesto. I did just meet her for the first time yesterday, and he met her for the first time this morning."

"If that's so, why did you go to her

place right after talking to me?"

"Simple, you wouldn't tell me why you were interested, and I was curious. Look, inspector, Ernesto and I are retired with time on our hands. We just wanted to know what was going on. In addition, Abigail's a neighbor. If she's in some kind of trouble, it wouldn't be right for me to stand by and do nothing."

Williams' face got a calculating look. His stare bored through Ed.

"So, what did she tell you?" he asked.

That brought Ed up short. If he told Williams that they hadn't asked about him, it would arouse his suspicions, and make them look guilty of something. On the other hand, he was still not quite ready to trust him, so he decided to go on the offensive by changing the subject.

"How did you know we went to see her? I seriously doubt that any of the other residents would have told you, so that means you must have been following us."

"You are one stubborn old man," Williams said. He had a half smile on his face. "I was in the parking lot when you two came out of the building. I was just about to drive away when I noticed that you were checking license plates. That's not exactly what I'd call normal activity, in fact, it was highly suspicious. So I just ducked down so you wouldn't see me, and when you left, I discretely followed you."

"So," Ernesto said. "You were in an unmarked vehicle. Why is that?"

"Not that it's any of your business, but many of the vehicles we use have regular plates. Sometimes we'd rather not advertise our presence."

"Okay, I'll grant you that," Ed said. "But, why would you follow us to that shopping mall? Are you investigating us for something?"

"Should I be?" Williams raised his brows and a half smile creased his face. "For your information, I didn't follow you. Someone else saw you and passed the information to me."

It was clear to Ed from the set of the man's jaw and the steely look in his eyes that he wasn't going to say more. It was also clear that something big was going on, and he and

Ernesto were in the middle of it.

"Fine, so we went to The Mail Box," Ed said. "That's not exactly a crime."

"Yeah, a lot of people use places like that because sometimes the Post Office isn't convenient," Ernesto added.

"That's a strange attitude for a former postal employee," Williams said.

"Didn't say I liked it, just pointing out the facts."

"You still haven't said why it's of concern," Ed said.

"I . . . let's just say that facility is of interest in an ongoing investigation and leave it at that. Are either of you customers of The Mail Box?"

They both shook their heads.

"Good," he said. "If you'll take my advice, you'll keep it that way, and you'll stay away from it. Now, do you mind telling me what you talked to Belmont Bosworth about?"

"Nothing really," Ed said. "That is, we didn't really have what you might call a conversation. He just asked us why we were at The Mail Box, but like you, he wouldn't tell us why he wanted to know. Who is

Mr. Bosworth, anyway?"

Williams seemed to be considering the question. Finally, he shrugged. "I guess there's no harm in telling you that," he said. "Belmont Bosworth, known on the street as B.B., is one of the most notorious gangsters in the DC metro area. He's into just about every racket you could imagine, and not someone you want to be mixed up with."

"Yeah, I sort of got that from the big goon he sent to fetch us," Ernesto said. "Would you know why he'd be interested in a mail drop place?"

"No," Williams said. A bit too quickly, Ed thought. "I have no idea at all, but take my advice, stay away from him, and please, stay away from The Mail Box."

"Sure, no problem," Ed said. "You know, it'd be helpful if we knew what this was all about."

Williams stood and headed for the door without responding. He opened the door, letting in a blast of frigid air, and turned to face them, his expression stern. "Thank you for you for your time, gentlemen, and don't forget what I said." He then pulled the door shut, leaving Ed and Ernesto standing there staring at it.

It also left Ed more determined than ever to find out what the hell was going on.

NINE

"Now, what the hell do you think that was all about?" Ernesto asked as they went back to the sofa.

"You got me," Ed responded. "Whatever it is, though, it's important, and just possibly dangerous. This is beginning to look like more than a simple case of a young man avoiding his irritating grandmother. I have a feeling that young Mr. Levi Crumley is in some kind of trouble."

"That's putting it mildly, amigo. If the Postal Inspection Service is involved it's some pretty serious doo doo."

Ed ran his hand over his hair, looking confused. "Why would they be involved anyway? The Mail Box isn't part of the U.S. Postal Service."

"True, but I'll bet you some of the stuff that goes through there gets handled by the Post Office at some point, and that's all it takes for the postal inspectors to latch on-to it like a pit bull on a piece of raw beef."

He went on to explain that the Postal Inspection Service, originally organized by Benjamin Franklin right after the Revolutionary War, was as old as the Post Office itself. The early inspectors, he said, were called surveyors, and their main job was to protect the mail and audit post offices. During the War of 1812, surveyors spied on British fleet movements on the Potomac River, and they kept the mail moving during the Civil War. After the Civil War, swindles using the mail began to proliferate, Congress passed the Mail Fraud Act, and gave the postal inspectors jurisdiction. Postal Inspectors were essential to the capture of the Unabomber, and are heavily involved in investigation of child pornography via the Internet. They get involved in email fraud schemes as well.

"So, you're saying that Abigail's grandson's probably involved in some kind of mail fraud?"

Ernesto looked glum. "Let's hope so," he said. "But, with this gangster involved, it could even be child pornography, and if that's the case, he's looking at a long prison sentence, one that he's not likely to survive."

"Huh?"

"Convicts might be the scum of the earth, but they take a pretty dim view of other convicts who abuse children. Few of the people convicted of that kind of offense live long in prison."

"Damn," was all Ed could say.

"And then there's the possibility that this might be terrorism related. You know that ever since September 11, everybody's been paranoid about terrorists. If this is related to that, the kid could end up in Guantanamo or something."

"Double damn," Ed said.

"So, compadre, what do we do now?"

"We need to go talk to Abigail," Ed said. He looked glum. "I think she's been holding out on us."

"We gonna do that tonight?"

"No, it can wait until morning. Say, you want to stay for supper?"

"And eat tuna fish and salad? I don't think so. You got any pork sausage?"

TEN

Ed found a package of pork sausages in his freezer, which he defrosted and baked in his oven until they were golden brown and the kitchen was filled with the maple-flavored aroma.. He dumped the can of tuna into the salad he'd made earlier, which Ernesto then agreed to eat, and they washed that down with two bottles of Corona each.

After supper they sat in the living room for another hour, drinking Jim Beam over ice and talking about everything but the case, which Ed insisted on, claiming it helped him to solve problems better if he let his unconscious mind work on them. Ernesto kidded him that he was just doing that because he had no idea what they were doing, which he grudgingly admitted *was* the main reason, and they continued drinking until the bottle was empty.

Ernesto left at 10:30, promising to be back the next morning bright and early, which Ed knew meant bright and *early*..

After his friend left, Ed sat alone on the sofa for half an hour, and sitting there alone he couldn't avoid thinking about the situation, and the more he thought about it the angrier he became.

There were many things that irritated him. People who cut in line at the register in the super market, idiots who changed lanes in front of you without using their turn signal, and inconsiderate people who parked illegally in the handicapped spaces got under his skin. But, the thing that bothered him more than anything else was being treated like a naïve idiot, to have people try to fool him as if he'd just hopped off the onion truck. And, that seemed to sum this whole situation up just nicely. Abigail Crumley was holding something back, which made no sense. She either wanted to find her grandson or she didn't. He had to assume she did, or why else would she offer to pay him five thousand dollars. But, if she did, why was she not telling him everything? His mind kept going around in circles on that one, but he couldn't figure it out. Then, there was Williams, the postal inspector. Ed understood the need for security. He had, after all, worked in the Pentagon for years, a place where *everything* is classified, and people are always talking about 'need-to-know.' But, dammit, he *needed* to know what was going on. No, strike that, he thought. I just *want* to know because I'm sort of in the middle of it. But, it's not fair of Williams to dangle a juicy puzzle like this in my face and not at least give me a hint of what's going on. Finally, there was the gangster, Bosworth. Despite his oily, unctuous behavior, his approach to Ed and Ernesto had been meant to intimidate, and what pissed Ed was that it had worked. That big guy was scary, and Bosworth, despite his small size, was even scarier.

He went to bed with all this on his mind, and woke up still angry. When he left his house and met Ernesto coming across the street, he was still royally pissed.

"Hey, amigo," Ernesto called out as he approached. "You look like you got up on the wrong side of the bed this morning." Ed's response was a growling sound like an angry dog about to pounce. "Okay, forget I said anything. Maybe some chow will make you feel better."

It didn't though. By the time they'd eaten their way through pancakes, sausage, hash browns, juice, and two cups of coffee each, Ed still had a sour look on his face. But, he felt like talking.

"You're right, Ernesto," he said. "I'm upset. In fact, I'm pissed off."

"Dare I ask what's got you so ticked off?"

Ed raised a finger. "First, I'm certain Abigail's playing me . . . us. She hasn't told us the whole story about her grandson." He added a finger. "Second, I'm pissed at that cop, Williams. He's treating us like we're a couple of kids. Something's going on, and thanks to Abigail, we've been thrust into it. He knows what it is, but won't tell us. And, finally, I'm a bit steamed at that thug, Bosworth. Who the hell does he think he is, anyway? Everyone associated with this mess is treating us like a couple of doddering, insignificant old fools. That just makes me mad."

Ernesto took a sip of coffee and made a face. "Yuck, coffee's cold already. Hey, I know it's a bummer, especially Abigail. She shouldn't do whatever it is she's done, but I think when we talk to her she'll see the light." He shoved the cup aside. "As for Williams, you know how it is. He's probably got some big investigation going, and is under pressure from his bosses. Last thing he needs is for two amateurs like us dipping our wicks in his tallow. And, I think this dude, Bosworth's just trying to show us that his is bigger than ours."

Ed shook his head. "What the hell does that even mean? Danged if sometimes you don't sound like some yokel from below the Mason-Dixon Line." He shrugged. "I know

Williams can't tell us everything, but with this gangster involved, he could tell us a *little*. As for Bosworth, I'm just gonna try and forget about him."

"Yeah, but you know Williams won't tell us anything. That ain't gonna happen. So, what do we do, back off?"

"Come on," Ed said. "You know me better than that. When someone's keeping something from me, I just have to find out what it is. Backing off is not my style."

"I kinda knew you were gonna say that. So, what do we do next?"

Ed looked down at his own coffee. A thin film of scum had formed on the surface. "Well, the coffee's gone cold, so we might as well pay a call on Abigail."

Tucked into their jackets against the chilly air, they walked briskly from the community center, across between the apartment buildings to Abigail's street. Ed had rung her doorbell twice before she finally opened the door. When she saw them, her eyes narrowed to slits and her lips turned down in a grimace of distaste.

"You find my grandson yet?" she asked.

"Aren't you going to invite us in?" Ed asked, returning curtness for curtness.

She looked as if he'd stepped on her corns, but stepped back and let them enter. They trooped across the room and sat on the sofa without waiting for an invitation to sit. She followed and sat on the uncomfortable looking metal chair opposite.

"You didn't answer my question," she said.

"The answer is no," Ed said. "And, until you start being up front with us, it's probably gonna remain no."

"What do you mean? I told you everything I know about Levi."

"You didn't tell us your grandson might be involved in some kind of mail fraud scheme . . . or worse."

She opened her mouth, and then snapped it shut, and looked down at her feet.

Ernesto snapped his fingers. "Now, that is what we call a tell in poker," he said.

"A what?" She looked wide eyed

at him.

"It's a signal that you're with-holding something," Ed said. "Or that you're lying or about to lie."

"How dare you call me a li-ar!"

"No, Abigail, how dare *you*. You sent us off on a wild goose chase, and you knew that your nephew's involved in something illegal. Did you also know there's a gangster looking for him?"

"No, I didn't," she answered quickly. Too quickly, Ed thought. Another lie.

"Come on, Abigail, if you want us to help you, you've got to stop bull shitting us."

She puffed out her cheeks, an indignant look in her eyes, but Ed just stared levelly at her. Then, like a balloon with a pinprick, she slowly deflated. She looked hollowly at him.

"Okay, I g-guess I didn't tell you everything," she said in a small voice. "B-but, Levi's a good boy. He'd never hurt anyone."

"So, what *is* he involved in?"

"Uh, he just delivers stuff for that mail place is all," she said.

Ed blinked. The Mail Box clerk

had said Levi Crumley worked as a freelancer. Either he was lying or Abigail was.

"You're saying he actually worked *for* The Mail Box?"

Her head bobbed up and down. "Yeah, sort of, I mean, indirectly I guess you could say he works for Mr. Bosworth, because Mr. Bosworth owns The Mail Box, and when they need stuff delivered, Levi takes his van over and picks it up and delivers it."

That much Ed figured was true, but it still didn't answer the question of *who* her grandson actually worked for.

"The gangster, B.B. Bosworth owns The Mail Box?"

He noticed that her eyes flickered briefly at the mention of the gangster's name. She shook her head.

"I don't know nothing about him being a gangster," she said. "Far as I know, he owns a bunch of 'em around here."

"Does Levi deliver packages for any of the others?"

"No, just know the mail place on

Georgia Avenue, the fellow who runs it would give Levi packages to deliver about once a week."

"Who did he deliver these . . . packages to?"

"I have no idea." Again, she spoke too quickly, telling Ed that she was lying. "We never talked much about his work. I mean, as long as he was making his own money and staying out of trouble, I didn't care. I was a little worried when he moved out, but he seemed to be doing okay on his own, so I thought that was a good thing until he didn't come around like he usually did."

Abigail was been more voluble than ever, but she'd been lying about the gangster, and it left Ed wondering just what else she was either lying about or withholding. He was getting a real itchy feeling at the base of his skull about the whole set up. In fact, thinking about the word 'set up' made him feel like a bug at the end of a pin.

"I have to tell you, Abigail," Ed said. "I'm not feeling a warm feeling of trust right now."

"What do you mean?"

"I mean, I know you're still holding something back. I don't know what it is, but I'll figure it out."

"Does that mean you're not gonna help me find Levi?"

Ed thought that if he was smart he'd tell her that's exactly what it meant. But, he wouldn't. He wouldn't because if by some remote chance the kid was being forced to do something wrong, he'd never forgive himself for not doing all he could to help, and while he was sure Abigail was keeping something from him, it could be she was just trying to protect her grandson. In addition, he just couldn't resist wanting to know what was going on. That was his one big failing. He couldn't keep his nose out of other people's business.

"No, I'll still try and find him for you," he said. "But, when all this is over, you and I are going to sit down and have a long talk about the importance of being honest with your friends."

"You . . . you think of me as a friend?"

He thought about that for all of

ten seconds before responding. "You're a neighbor, and I've always been taught to help neighbors. But, yes, until you prove otherwise, I also think of you as a friend."

For the first time since he'd met her in the community center Sunday morning, Abigail Crumley smiled. It didn't make her beautiful by any stretch of even a drug-addled imagination it did make her look a little less like a witch.

ELEVEN

They left Abigail sitting on her couch staring at the walls. Outside on the sidewalk, Ernesto grasped Ed's fore-arm, stopping him in his tracks.

"Okay, dude, what're we gonna do now?" he asked.

"We're going to pay another visit to our friend at The Mail Box."

"But, Williams told us to stay away from there." Ernesto's brow crinkled.

Ed scratched his head. Then, he smiled and patted his friend's shoulder.

"You know how it is with us senior citizens, amigo," he said. "We have terrible memories. I completely forgot he told us that."

"That what you're gonna tell him when he hauls our asses off to jail?"

Ed just smiled, shrugged. "Let's take your car today, okay."

"Well, at least that's an improvement. Let's go."

Ernesto drove much faster than Ed, so they were in the parking lot of the mall in five minutes less time than they'd taken with Ed driving. In a pickup, the effect was unsettling.

"Park several shops down from The Mail Box," Ed said.

Ernesto nodded and drove to the area in front of Giant Foods. They got out and walked back to The Mail Box, staying close to the shop walls, not so much to escape detection as to stay as much out of a brisk wind that had sprung up as possible.

The same clerk, with the same pimply face, stood idly behind the counter. He looked up at the sound of the bell when they entered. There was no hint of recognition in his eyes.

"Yeah, what can I do for you?" he asked.

"You don't remember us, do you?" Ed asked.

Pimply face picked at his over-bite and looked indolently at Ed. "Naw, should I?"

Ernesto leaned over the counter, putting his face close to Pimply face, and instantly regretted it as he was hit in the face with the kid's noxious inhalation, an odor that was a combination of onion, stale beer, and dirty gym socks. He pulled back slightly, but raised his hand and grabbed the kid's collar. "Do you remember this?" he asked as he hauled him over the counter.

"Urgh, urk," Pimply face said. His face started turning purple. "You're, urk, the two old dudes who came in the other day looking for Levi Crumley . . . right?"

Ernesto eased the pressure and lowered the kid back until his feet were on the floor, but hung onto his collar.

"Good answer," he said. He turned to Ed and smiled. "Sometimes you just have to ask the question the right way."

Ed stepped up beside Ernesto.

Pimply face's eyes were bouncing from side to side as he watched one then the other, and his Adam's apple was doing a little dance.

"W-what do you want?" he asked.

"For starters," Ed said. "I want to know why you called that gangster, Belmont Bosworth and led him to us before."

The kid's face went fish belly white and his Adam's apple dance got jigglier. His side-to-side eye movement doubled in speed. "B-bosworth . . . I d-don't know nobody b-by that name."

When a person's under stress, it's hard to read body language, and having been hauled over the counter by Ernesto, Pimply face was no doubt stressed out. Nonetheless, his body reactions to Bosworth's name seemed pretty clear. He not only knew Bosworth, but he was scared shitless of him. Ed decided to change the line of questioning.

'Let's get back to Levi Crumley," he said. "Did he come in on a regular schedule to pick up packages, or did you call to let him know there was stuff to pick up?"

Pimply face seemed to be thinking over the question—probably wondering how much he could safely share without running afoul of Bosworth, Ed thought. Then, he looked at Ernesto, who was still hanging onto his collar, and he swallowed hard. "Uh, I'd give him a call whenever there was stuff," he said, apparently deciding the threat with a hand near his throat was to be feared more than the one not present.

"And, how often did you call him?"

"Like I told you last time, about once a week."

"When was the last pickup?"

Pimply face hesitated. Probably getting into dangerous territory, Ed thought.

"Week before last," Pimply face finally said.

"I don't suppose you'll be willing to tell us who these packages were for?"

"No way, man, that'd cost me my . . . job."

"You want I should rough him up some more, Ed?" Ernesto asked.

Ed wouldn't have thought the kid's face could get any paler, but he gulped and all the color that was left drained from his slack jaws.

"C-come on, man, gimme a break, okay? I ain't done nothing to you guys. I'm just trying to make a living here."

That wasn't precisely true, Ed thought. The little turd had ratted them out to the gangster Bosworth. On the other hand, that behemoth Bosworth had sent after them could intimidate a bulldozer, so he couldn't really blame the kid for being scared.

"No," Ed said. "Let him go . . . this time." He waved a finger at Pimply face, who was breathing so fast he looked like he was about to hyperventilate. "But, if you cross us again, we'll be back, and you won't like what happens if we do that. You understand?"

"Y-yeah, I get it. I don't know you dudes."

Ernesto let go of his collar and Pimply face fell back against the shelf, still gulping for air and staring at them.

With one last steely look at him,

Ed spun on his heels and headed for the exit.

"Come on, Ernesto, let's get out of here. This place smells like wet dog."

Outside, as they headed back to Ernesto's car, he looked askance at Ed. "You know that little shit's gonna call his gangster buddy, right?"

Ed nodded. "Yeah, I figure he's on the phone as we speak."

Ernesto shrugged. "Oh, okay. Just wanted to make sure you understood that."

Charles Ray

TWELVE

Ernesto drove out of the parking lot at the end down from The Mail Box, looking in his rearview mirror constantly. When he reached the street, he darted in front of an oncoming delivery van whose driver leaned on his horn and swung his fists, swung hard left, cutting off a young woman in a Prius, who gave him the finger, and pressed hard on the gas until he was ten miles over the 35MPH speed limit. Ed pressed his palms against the dash, and prayed silently, hoping they wouldn't encounter some idiot pulling onto Georgia Avenue in front of them because at the speed he was driving, stopping before a crash would be a pipedream. He also had some doubts about the ability of a pickup to safely navigate at the speed Ernesto was driving, but kept his mouth shut to avoid distracting him.

Three-quarters of a mile from the shopping mall they came to a stretch of Georgia Avenue that's in that part of Montgomery County that can't decide whether it's urban, suburban, or rural, so it has elements of all three.

The traffic was surprisingly light for the time of day, with a large tanker truck receding in the distance far ahead of them, and two unidentified cars in the rear view mirrors. The collection of gas stations, warehouses, and fenced in construction storage lots next to the shopping mall had given way to wooded areas, with small trees and scrub brush near the highway giving way to thick stands of mixed deciduous and evergreens farther back. They passed a small, single story house on the left across the street from a modest church. The house, shaped like a cracker box, had a peeling black shingle roof and yellow siding. The window shutters were weather-stained black and a couple hung precariously. The yard around the house was a combination of hard-packed brown earth and knee-high grass in need of mowing, and was decorated with two rotting tires and a banged up, rusted out pickup with the two front tires missing. The church was gray stone with a small steeple and arched stained glass windows. The area around the church building was neatly trimmed, though the grass was brown from the cold. A portable signboard sat at the entrance way, its stick on letters saying, 'Mount Zion Presbyterian Church, Ye Shall Know the Truth, and the Truth Shall set You Free' at the top, with two lines of the angular Korean characters and two lines of Chinese characters below that.

Past that, the land emptied out. Ragged bushes and the naked trunks of small trees poked up through gray-green grass on both sides stretching back to the darkness of a forest on land belonging to the county that hadn't been opened up to developers.

The tanker truck had disappeared around a bend in the road ahead, and one of the cars behind had turned off. The remaining car, that Ed could see in the right rear-view mirror was a large dark sedan, was getting closer. He looked at the speedometer. Ernesto was doing 60, the speed limit was 45. The driver of that car had to be driving like a bat out of hell to be closing on them, he thought. The sight brought to mind the time he'd spent in Germany in the late 60s when he was a young corporal in the army, watching German drivers drive like speed demons to catch up with and pass anything that had the gall to be driving in front of them. On more than one occasion he'd seen the scrap metal left after the driver of a tiny Volkswagen had misjudged clearance and cut in too soon after passing a larger vehicle. *I wonder if I should tell Ernesto to slow down and let this idiot pass us.* He immediately discarded that idea. Like the German drivers he remembered, Ernesto wasn't one to let anyone pass him. He would risk a speeding ticket instead. Ed crossed his fingers and hoped for the best.

The empty land was suddenly replaced on both sides of Georgia Avenue by the sandy brown color of 12-foot-high concrete sound baffles set back ten feet from the slightly sloped shoulder of the road. The thick concrete slabs set in slight zig-zag patterns, they were there to block traffic noises for the over-priced suburban housing behind them. Ed looked in the rearview mirror and noted that the car behind them was even closer now; close enough for him to see that it was a dark blue Cadillac CT6 and that there were two people in the front seat. Oh, and that it showed no sign of slowing down.

"Uh, Ernesto," he said. "We got a car coming up behind us fast."

Ernesto had a death grip on the steering wheel, and kept glancing up at the rearview mirror.

"Yeah, I see him. Looks like he wants to play chicken or something. He ain't slowing down at all."

"I don't like this," Ed said. "If he rams into us with that thing, we're in trouble. Maybe you should pull over and let him go by."

"Nah, I don't think so. If I slow down to pull over, he might not notice and rear-end us. The way this thing's balanced, we might flip over. As much as I hate to admit it, I'd feel safer in that ugly SUV of yours right now."

"So, what do we do?"

Ernesto's eyes flickered forward, and his grip on the wheel tightened. "Hang on," he said, and whipped the wheel suddenly to the right.

Ed felt a suddenly pull to the left as the Chevy did a 90 degree right turn toward the gap in the sound baffles, saved from slamming into Ernesto only by the tightening of the seat belts. The tires screamed as they slid on the concrete, and the car shimmied and slid sidewise before the tires gripped and shot them forward. The Chevy's engine roared in protest. Ed heard, 'pop-pop-pop-pop!', followed by the crashing sound of breaking glass as the rear window of the cab dissolved into a shower of flying glass and four holes appeared in the windshield in front of him. It took his brain a few seconds to process what he was seeing. Fortunately, except for a few pellets of flying glass from the rear window, they hadn't been hit. *Somebody up there's looking out for us*, he thought. Ernesto still had the wheel in a death grip. His eyes, though, were on the four holes in the windshield.

The Cadillac had stopped on Georgia Avenue at the opening in the baffles, and Ed could, by craning around in his seat, see through the opening of the rear window, a large dark man getting out and raising his right arm. The man was holding what looked to Ed to be a very large, very deadly looking pistol, and he was aiming it at them.

"Look out," Ed shouted, but Ernesto had just looked in the rear-view mirror.

Before the man could shoot, Ernesto jerked the wheel again, and they took a right turn down a suburban street, engine still roaring, doing 60MPH between expensive colonial style houses. They were fortunate that there were no pedestrians, especially kids, on the street.

Ernesto drove one block and

took a left turn, slowing to the 25MPH speed limit, constantly checking the rearview mirror.

"They shot at us," Ed said, his voice shaking. "You think they'll follow us in here."

In the distance they heard the sound of sirens. Ed could imagine that at least a dozen shocked home-owners had called 911.

"Nah, I don't think so," Ernesto said. He twisted around and looked at the gaping opening that had been his car's rear window. "Darn, wish we'd brought your car this time."

Ed's phone rang. He pulled out and looked at the face—a 301 area code but no name. He answered.

"Hello," he said.

"Mr. Lazenby," a deep, creepy sounding voice said. "Consider what just happened a warning. Stay away from The Mail Box. Next time we won't miss."

The connection was broken before Ed could respond.

"Who was that?" Ernesto asked.

"I think that was Mr. Bosworth or his representative," Ed said. "He doesn't want us to find Levi Crumley anymore, I think."

"So, what do we do now?"
"We wait until the police arrive."

Charles Ray

THIRTEEN

Ed let his heart rate slow down for a few seconds before pulling out his cell phone and dialing 911. He gave the 911 operator their location as best he could and told her what had happened. As soon as he stopped talking, he was told that the police were on their way.

Three Montgomery County Police squad cars, lights flashing, and officers jumping out with weapons drawn, arrived four minutes later.

"Damn," Ernesto said. "That was quick. They'd never get to PVC that quick."

"Look around," Ed said. "This is a rich neighborhood. I imagine someone here heard the shots and called, and even if they're responding to my call, folks with money get faster service than us middle income types."

"Get out of the car with your hands up," one of the cops shouted, aiming his service weapon at Ed through the window.

As soon as they exited the car, they were told in loud, commanding voices to lie face down on the ground with their hands behind their heads; an uncomfortable position given the coldness of the macadam surface. One officer gave them a complete pat down while the other five kept them covered, and only after they were cleared as not being armed were they were allowed to stand. The officers kept their weapons out, though pointed at the ground, while the officer who'd searched them checked the cab of the pickup. Ed asked permission to remove Williams' card from his pocket, which he gave to the beefy cop standing nearest. After looking at it, he appraised them carefully with his steely blue eyes.

"Why're you giving me the card of a U.S. Postal Inspector?" he asked.

"If you'll call him, he can explain things," Ed said.

"He can explain why you came tearing into a community with the back window of your car shot out?" The cop had a disbelieving look on his wind-burned face.

"Yes, as a matter of fact he can."

Still looking skeptical, the cop returned to his car and spoke into the mike. After a brief conversation, he returned to face Ed and Ernesto.

"HQ called this guy Williams," the cop said. "He's on the way. In the meantime, how about you tell me what the hell happened."

They alternated in relating what had happened, leaving out any reference to their visit to The Mail Box and their belief that that was why they'd been attacked.

"Did you get a look at anyone in the other car?"

"No," Ernesto said. "I was busy driving."

"And, I was ducking," Ed said.

"How about a license plate number?"

Ernesto shook his head, but Ed

said, "I didn't get a clear look, but it was a Maryland plate, and the last two numbers were 86. Sorry I can't tell you more. It all happened so fast."

"And, you're sure you only heard four shots?"

They nodded. Ernesto clutched at his chest and leaned against the side of the car. Ed grabbed his shoulder. "You okay, amigo?"

The cop rushed forward. "Sir, are you okay? You're not having a—"

Ernesto waved them both away. "No, I'm not having a heart attack if that's what you're worried about. Just gas pains from what I ate earlier and all this excitement."

"Maybe you should sit down," Ed said. "Is that okay, officer?"

A worried look creased the cop's face.

"Yeah, I guess that's okay."

As Ernesto eased himself down to the steps of the pickup and leaned back with his hands folded across his stomach, Ed stood there looking down at him. The cop walked back to his colleagues and spoke with them. Except for his partner, who stood by their squad car, his weapon now holstered, the others got into their cars and drove away. The cop came back.

"We have a BOLO out on the car based on your description," he said. "But, it's probably long gone by now. This guy Williams said he was on the way, and we were to hold you here until he arrived, but he didn't say I couldn't ask questions."

"Sure, officer, go ahead," Ed said.

"Do either of you have any idea why someone would want to shoot at you?"

Ed and Ernesto shared a glance. "No, we have no idea," Ed said.

"Yeah, they just started shooting at us," Ernesto said. "At first, I thought it was a rock through the window, but then I saw the bullet holes in the front."

"You're lucky. If the guy shooting at you'd been a better shot, you wouldn't be talking to me right now."

His partner, who was now in the squad car talking on the radio, called him over, and he walked back to his squad car and got in. The two cops were deep in conversation when a black Chevy Suburban with DC plates pulled in beside the cop car.

Joshua Williams got out and walked to the cop car. He showed his credentials to the driver, nodded, and walked over to Ed.

"You two just can't stay out of trouble, can you?" he said before Ed could speak.

Ernesto looked up at him. "You're not blaming us for this are you?"

Williams rubbed at the stubble he still hadn't shaved and his still bloodshot eyes blazed. "You're fucking 'A' I am," he nearly shouted. "I told you two to stay away from The Mail Box, but you just had to go back anyway. Now, you're getting shot at and upsetting the residents of an upscale housing development, not to mention getting the county cops involved." He balled up his fists and hit them against his thighs.

Ed held his hands up in a placating gesture.

"Okay, our bad," he said. "But, we had a good reason for going back there."

Williams shook his head and growled. "I do not want to hear it. You were not supposed to go back there under any circumstances. I oughta haul both your asses in for interfering in the conduct of a federal investigation."

"Well," Ed said. "If we knew what was going on, maybe we wouldn't have gone back."

"Yeah, you keep us in the dark, and we stumble into trouble," Ernesto said.

"Oh, shut up, both of you." Williams ran a hand through his hair, which looked as if he'd forgotten to comb it when he got out of bed. "God, I hope I'm not this much trouble when I get old."

"We're not old, just experienced," Ed said. "Now, could you please tell us what's so important that this Bosworth character would have some try and shoot us?"

"You sure it was Bosworth's goons?" Williams shook his head. "Of course, it had to be. Okay, dammit, we'll go back to your place and we'll talk, and then hopefully I can get you two off my back."

"Okay," Ernesto said. "I'll follow you."

"No the hell you won't," Williams said. "That pickup's a crime scene, and it's not going anywhere until the forensics guys go over it. The police will guard it until they finish. You can ride with me." He turned and walked away.

Ed shrugged and followed. Grumbling, Ernesto got out and followed him. "Oh well, I've always wanted to ride in one of those things," he said, nodding at the Suburban. "Does it go fast?"

Williams gave him an evil look.

FOURTEEN

The ride to Ed's house was silent, and frosty. Williams kept his eyes on the road and refused to respond to Ernesto's efforts at conversation. Reading the tea leaves, and not wanting to make the situation worse, Ed kept his mouth shut.

When they arrived, Ed took everyone's jackets and hung them in the closet near the entrance.

"Why don't you two make yourselves comfortable," he said. "While I go and brew a pot of coffee."

When he came back ten minutes later carrying a coffee urn and three ceramic mugs on a plastic tray he'd 'borrowed' from the community dining facility, Ernesto and Williams were sitting on opposite ends of the couch glaring at each other.

"You two discuss anything interesting while I was gone," he said in a vain effort to lighten the mood.

"I tried explaining to this hard head that we didn't do anything wrong," Ernesto said.

"Who are you calling hard head, old man?" Williams' face turned red.

"Stop calling me old man."

"You—"

"Stop it, both of you," Ed said, sitting the tray on the coffee table. "Now, Inspector Williams, you should really learn that it's considered insulting to harp on age, or call people in this community old. We're kind of sensitive on the subject."

Williams looked down and clasped his hands together. "Sorry," he murmured.

"You should be—"

"That's enough, Ernesto," Ed cut his friend off. "He's right, you know. We should never have gone back to that place." Williams gave Ernesto an 'I told you so' smile. "But, inspector, if you'd just leveled with us in the first place, we might not have gone."

Williams looked abashed at first, then his eyes widened. "Whoa," he said. "Okay, maybe I should have told you what was going on, but you lied to me first when you said you didn't know Abigail Crumley."

Ed was forced to admit that the postal inspector had him on that one. He covered his embarrassment by sitting in the chair facing the sofa and pouring coffee. He then took his time passing the mugs across, and killed further seconds by blowing on his own several times before taking a sip.

"I didn't exactly *lie* to you, inspector," he said when he'd regained his composure. "I did just meet Abigail for the first time that day. I did what you did, though, and I withheld information." He then proceeded to explain Abigail's request that he find her grandson. "So, you see, since you didn't tell me why you were interested in her in the first place, I saw no need to tell you about young Levi."

It was now Williams turn to look abashed.

"Okay, okay, I guess I can understand that," he said. "Here's the deal; what I'm about to tell you goes no further, you understand?" Ed and Ernesto nodded their agreement. "We've been investigating a big fraud operation for the past six months. It's nationwide, and has been using these mail drop places to try and avoid getting on our radar. Unfortunately, they're so successful, they've attracted victims from places that don't have such places, and a few of the responses to the scam have spent a portion of their transit in the U.S. Postal system—all we need to get involved."

"Just like I told you," Ernesto said.

Ed ignored him and turned to Williams. "What kind of scheme, and how is Abigail Crumley involved?" Ed asked.

"It's one of those 'work from home and get rich' schemes," Williams said. "You send money, in this case twenty bucks, to an address, and they're supposed to send you this kit telling you how to set up your own home-based business. In return for their twenty dollars, the victims get a little 12-page pamphlet that offers a more complete course of instruction and starter kit for a hundred dollars."

"And, people actually fall for this?" Ed shook his head.

"Unfortunately, too many do. Because a lot of people never report it, we don't have good figures, but we estimate over a billion dollars a year gets sucked up by scammers. And now, with the Internet, it's only gotten worse."

"Okay, so these people are getting twenty dollars from some idiot, and they're giving them a cheap pamphlet in return," Ed said. "That's unethical, but I don't see how you could really prosecute anyone for it."

"You're right. Even though the pamphlet only costs the scammers less than a dollar, say a buck fifty with envelope and postage, technically it'd be hard to prove fraud, despite the fact that they're getting about two thousand responses a week through the Georgia Avenue drop alone. It's the follow-on, though, that's outright fraud. When people send in the hundred bucks, that's the last they hear from these guys. About ten percent of the people who send in the twenty end up signing on for the hundred dollar package."

Ed had been doing the math in his head as Williams spoke. "Wow, that's almost fifty thousand dollars a week this place is raking in. And, you say there are others?"

"Hell yes," Williams said. "They have five others in the greater metro area, and they're all under the control of B.B. Bosworth."

"So, where does Abigail come in?"

Two circles of pink blossomed on Williams' cheeks. "Well, I wasn't being quite up front with you there," he said. "It's actually her grandson we're interested in. I was just hoping to get a lead on him by going through her."

Ed regarded him through narrowed slits. Then, he shrugged. "Ah ha, I see," he said. "Instead of aiming directly at your target, you applied offset, and aimed at where it would be at some point in the future."

"Huh?" Ernesto and Williams said in unison.

Ed smiled. "It's something the missile guys I knew when I worked in the Pentagon taught me," he said. "Because of the earth's rotation, if you aim a missile on a north-south axis, you can't expect it to fly in a straight line, because by the time it reaches its target, that target will have moved because of rotation. So, it actually flies in a kind of curved line. It's similar to hunting. You lead a moving target so the target and the bullet arrive at the same place at the same time. So, the way I figure it, you don't know a lot about Levi Crumley, so your intent was to get a lead on him from his grandmother."

"Uh, yeah, without all the curved line and earth rotation mumbo jumbo, that's what I was planning."

"The curved line mumbo jumbo is called the Coriolis Effect," Ed said. "But, that's neither here nor there. You don't have a snowball's chance in hell of getting anything useful out of Abigail Crumley."

"Well, I wasn't exactly planning to talk to her directly. I was hoping to get information from her friends, and see it that might give me a lead on where Levi might be."

"Never work," Ernesto said.

"Why's that?"

"Because, except for me and Ed, and I'm not too sure about us, Abigail Crumley has no friends here at Potomac Valley Community."

"Shit, you mean I wasted all this time?"

"Maybe not," Ed said. "There still might be a way to make this work."

"How?" Williams looked hopeful.

"Well, Abigail still wants me to find her grandson. So, if you'll let us keep working on that it might help your investigation."

"I . . . don't know," Williams said. "My boss might not like me getting a couple of civilians involved, and besides, you've already seen, this can get pretty dangerous."

"Your boss doesn't have to know about us," Ed said. "We're just a couple of senior citizens trying to help a . . . friend. You can say that you warned us off."

"But, you're still gonna go looking for this kid?"

"That's about the size of it."

"And, you're gonna do this even if I tell you I don't want you becoming involved, right?"

Ernesto shrugged. Ed nodded.

Williams blew out a gust of air. "Man, I hope I don't regret doing this. You two old buzzards are gonna give me gray hair." He rose and dusted off the legs of his trousers. "Okay, you got my card. You keep me posted on everything you find out, and I mean *everything*, you got it?"

"Of course," Ed said.

"And, please, try not to get yourselves killed. If you do, I'll have a mountain of paperwork to do, and then I'll find myself guarding a post office in Nome, Alaska."

Charles Ray

FIFTEEN

After Williams left, Ed and Ernesto sat at the coffee table, sipping coffee and making plans.

"Okay, Sherlock," Ernesto said. "What do we do now?"

"I was thinking about that when Williams was talking," Ed responded. "Remember when we looked in Levi's room . . . all those boxes? I think we need to take a closer look at that stuff."

"How do you propose we do that? If you'll remember, Abigail didn't seem too happy to have us snooping around the last time."

"I was kind of hoping we'd be able to make use of that devilish charm of yours on this one," Ed said.

"Okay . . . whoa! You're not thinking what I think you're thinking, are you?"

Ed patted his friend's shoulder.

"I'd just need half an hour, an hour tops," he said. "Think of it as taking one for the team."

Ernesto's body quivered and he screwed his eyes shut. "Ye-e-ew, this is above and beyond. You're gonna owe me big time for this."

"Hey, I'll split the money Abigail promised me with you . . . fifty-fifty."

"Okay, I'll do it, but I feel so cheap."

"If you call that much money cheap, I'd like to be your agent when you take to the street."

"Aw, you know what I mean. Come on, let's do this before I change my mind."

They donned their jackets and headed out. A block from Abigail's house, Ed split off from his friend and walked to a small park, one of many in PVC designed and situated to allow the community's elderly residents to have places to stop frequently and rest when they walked about. The wooden bench slats were so cold they felt hot through the fabric of his trousers, so he just stood near a plastic ash receptacle—the parks were among the few public places where smoking was allowed—and walked in place to stay warm.

Their plan was relatively simple. Ernesto was to invite Abigail to join him in the community center for coffee where he would bring her up to date on what he and Ed had learned—leaving out any reference to the postal investigation or the gangster who liked shooting out the rear window of cars—and press her for more information on Levi's likely whereabouts. If necessary; and Ernesto shuddered each time Ed mentioned it; he was to flirt with her to keep her occupied. He was, upon leaving Abigail's house, to make sure the front door was not locked, so that Ed could get in.

Ed had chosen a park on the opposite side of Abigail's house from the community center that allowed him a view of her front door. He crossed his fingers and hoped that she wouldn't look in his direction and see him, but knew that most people tended to focus on the direction of their planned travel.

Sure enough, that's exactly what she did when she and Ernesto emerged from her front door three minutes after she'd let him in. She looked from Ernesto toward the community center and back to Ernesto. Ed noticed that her attention was mostly on Ernesto, and that she allowed him to close the door. *He complained, but he loves this stuff,* Ed thought. He allowed them to get out of sight before leaving the park and walking quickly down the sidewalk.

He walked straight up to her front door without looking right or left. At the door, he paused a second, and then pushed it open and stepped inside. Anyone walking by, or observing from any of the nearby houses would think he was visiting and the door had been opened for him by someone inside—or so he hoped.

Once inside, he closed and locked the door. He looked around the sterile living room, but saw nothing of interest. He briefly considered checking the kitchen, but the room he was most interested in was Levi's bedroom, so he made his way quickly across the living room and down the hall until he came to the closed door.

The room looked the same as he remembered, with boxes and large brown envelopes scattered about. He stopped in the center of the room and turned slowly, taking in the totality of the space. Nothing struck him, so he went to the closet and slid the doors aside. He held his nose against the wet dog smell that flowed out as the doors opened.

Inside the closet he found pretty much what he'd expected to find. Jeans, casual pants, casual shirts and sweaters hung haphazardly on an assortment of rusted wire and cracked wooden hangers. Not a suit, pair of dress pants or dress shirt in the bunch. Several of the pants were shiny at the knees and frayed at the cuff, and some of the shirts had missing buttons. On the floor were several pairs of scuffed shoes, mostly loafers, and a couple of pairs of running shoes that were run down at the heels. If Levi Crumley was making money from the scam he was participating in he certainly wasn't spending any of it on clothing.

He then crossed the room and did a quick survey of the dresser drawers, again almost choking from the odor that wafted up each time he opened a drawer. All he found was a motley assortment of underpants, mostly briefs, some in need of washing, a jumble of socks and some tee shirts with frayed necklines. On top of the dresser, the scattered envelopes of assorted sizes partly covered a rectangular watermark that was about four by nine inches.

All the closet and dresser told him was that Levi was something of a slob with zero fashion sense, in other words, a pretty typical twenty-something male.

Now, he turned his attention to the boxes and envelopes, beginning with those on the top of the dresser. Mostly, they were the nine by twelve sized manila envelopes with metal clasps for closing that are used for mailing documents without having to fold them, but a few were white business letter-size envelopes. The first few he picked up had never been used. Then, he picked up a letter-sized envelope that had the remnants of torn postage stamps and a Post Office cancellation mark. It looked as if someone had tried to remove the stamps, and had only been partially successful. Peering closely, he saw that the postmark was from three weeks earlier and had been done by a Post Office in Cedar Rapids, Iowa. It had been addressed in pen, but someone had taken an eraser to both sender and receiver's address, all but obliterating them except for two letters in the receiver's address. The 'g' and 'i', written in a spidery scrawl, were barely visible, and Ed couldn't tell whether they were part of the middle or end of a word. What it did do, though, was confirm for him that Levi was up to his chin in the scam. He folded the envelope and slipped it into his jacket pocket.

There were seven brown cardboard boxes on the floor. They were thirteen by ten inches in length and width and four inches deep, and had been sealed with brown packing tape. The tape had been ripped off hurriedly, and in a couple of cases balled up and stuffed into the boxes. None of them had any markings of any kind, and no indication of what they'd been used for, although Ed guessed that they'd been used to transport the envelopes. He was about to walk out when he noticed a greenish-white shape amidst the balled up tape in one of the boxes. He pulled the wad of tape out and began pulling it apart, revealing a crumpled twenty dollar bill, which he held carefully at the corner with his forefinger and thumb to keep from smearing any fingerprints that might be on it. Pressing it against the side of the box, he folded it and gingerly put it in his pocket with the envelope.

He made his way back to the living room. At the door, he peered through the narrow windows at the side to make sure the sidewalk outside was clear, and then let himself out, locking the door securely. Halfway back to his house he removed his cell phone and hit the speed dial for Ernesto's number.

"Yo, compadre," Ernesto answered on the first ring.

"It's done," Ed said. "Meet me at my house."

Charles Ray

SIXTEEN

"So, you got good evidence that her grandson's involved with these gangsters?" Ernesto asked.

"He's involved in the scam," Ed said, pointing to the envelope and banknote he'd placed on the coffee table. "Or, at least, he's aware of it. This leaves no doubt."

"You gonna turn that over to Williams?"

"Maybe, but first I think it's only fair that I talk to Abigail."

Ernesto looked puzzled. "Why? I mean, it's her grandson we need to be talking to . . . or at least, that Williams and his feds need to talk to."

Ed had been thinking about it

since leaving her house. Something was tickling at the back of his brain, a nagging thought that wanted to escape but couldn't find an exit. It was like having a dog door but your dumb mutt couldn't get the hang of how to use it, so he prances around wanting to go out and do his business—very annoying. He couldn't quite get it to come out into the light so he could know what it was, but he *knew* that somehow it involved Abigail Crumley, or her grandson. It would come, he knew. He just didn't know when, so for the time being, he'd continue plodding along.

"I'd just feel better if we talked to her first. She's not telling us something, and I think that something's key to solving this whole mess."

"Whew! I just spent forty minutes with her, and believe me, man, that's enough to last a lifetime. She never stopped talking."

"Did she say anything useful?"

Ernesto rolled his eyes. "Lemme put it another way; she never stopped complaining. I mean, that woman don't like nothing or nobody."

"Oh, I think she likes someone,"

Ed said.

"Like who?"

"You, of course, otherwise she wouldn't have talked to you so long. I think she might be sweet on you, old friend."

Ernesto grasped his chest. He looked as if he was about to have a heart attack. He frowned at Ed.

"Amigo, don't you ever say anything like that to me . . . ever again," he said.

"So, I take it you don't want to go with me to see her?"

"Ain't that what I just said? Hell, I'd rather go in for a colonoscopy."

"Okay, you can wait here for me if you want," Ed said. "This shouldn't take too long."

Ernesto was helping himself to the coffee when Ed pulled on his jacket and, was busy drinking it when Ed walked out the door.

It only took him a matter of minutes to reach Abigail's front door. She opened the door before the echo of the chimes had stopped. A look of confusion crossed her face when she saw Ed.

"Uh, what are you doing here?"

she asked. "I just talked to . . . your friend at the community center not twenty minutes ago."

"Do you mind if I come in, Abigail? There are some things we have to discuss," Ed said.

She hesitated to open the door further, her face screwed up in an unreadable expression. "Have you . . . located him yet? Is Levi okay?"

Ed swayed from side to side, shifting his weight from one foot to the other and slapping his upper arms. "It's really cold out here," he said. "How about I come in and we can discuss it?" To drive home his point, he exhaled, blowing a plume of white vapor in her direction.

Finally, she stepped back and opened the door for him to enter. He followed her toward the sofa, waiting for her to sit. When she sat on the sofa, he took the chair opposite her and leaned forward.

"Okay," she said. "What is it you want to talk about?"

"I'm going to lay it out for you, Abigail. You've been holding out on me about your grandson, and that's been a problem . . . more than just a problem, it's been pretty damn dangerous."

"What do you mean, danger-ous?"

He told her about getting shot at, causing her eyes to go round and her brows to shoot upwards, and about getting pushed face down on the cold concrete by the police.

"And, to add insult to injury, I find out that Levi's more than just a delivery boy for this operation."

"N-no, that's not right," she said. "M-my Levi just picks up and deliv-ers packages." She looked down at her hands twisted together in her lap.

"You're not being honest, Abi-gail." Then, Ed had an inspiration. "I think Levi's in some kind of trouble with this gangster, his boss." Her eyes flickered. "Like, maybe, he's been skimming money from him."

Her eyes flew wide and she put a hand to her trembling lips. "N-no . . . how did you . . . that's—"

"Stop it, Abigail. Your reaction told me that what I suspected is a fact. Now, it's time to be straight about this if you want me to help Levi."

"How did you find out?" she asked in a voice barely above a whisper.

"I have my ways of finding out things, remember?"

"Y-yes, I suppose you do," she said. "Okay, you're right. Levi's been working for that awful man, Bosworth, for two years now. He just picked up and delivered at first, but one day, one of the envelopes was torn, and it had cash in it." Her fingers were now tangled in her skirt, bunching it up between her hands, and her feet were beating a tattoo on the floor. "He figured Bosworth would never miss a few twenties here and there, after all, it was a bunch of envelopes, and he figured they all had money in them, so he took it. He started taking the money from five or six envelopes every shipment, and there was no problem. But, three weeks ago, he got word that Bosworth suspected someone in the operation was skimming, and he knew it was just a matter of time before they figured out it was him, so he ran away."

"He didn't tell you where he was going?"

She shook her head. "No, he just came in here all white-faced, near panic, and said he had to hide because B. B., that's what he calls that man, Bosworth, he said he was going to kill him. I didn't worry the first week, but when two weeks went by and I hadn't heard from him, I . . . I'm just so worried. I didn't know what else to do. You can understand why I didn't go to the police, right?"

"Yes, I can understand," he said. He reached forward and laid a hand on hers. "But, you know that when I find him, I'll have to report his location to the police."

"I-I suppose so. Oh, Ed, what am I to do? He's all I have. You have to find him."

"All I can tell you, Abigail, is to follow the words of the old saying, 'God, give me the serenity to accept the things I can't change, the courage to change the things I can change, and the wisdom to know the difference between the two."

"B-but, my Levi will go to jail."

"Probably," he said. "But, since he was just a delivery boy, they're likely to go easy on him. They're after the mastermind behind the operation, not low level people like Levi."

"Well, I guess going to jail's better than being dead," she said. "What else do you want to know to help you find him?"

Now, Ed thought, we're finally maybe getting somewhere. He talked to her for another half hour, asking probing questions about Levi's habits and hangouts, and at the end, he had a suspicion about where he was. But, before he could follow up on that, he needed to take care of another problem.

SEVENTEEN

"You've got to be kidding," Williams had said when Ed had first called him with his plan to go after Bosworth. After several minutes of arguing back and forth on the phone, he'd told Ed to wait until he arrived so they could discuss it in more detail.

He arrived still skeptical, but Ed wore him down. His desire to nab Bosworth eventually overcame his worry about the whole thing going south on them. His condition for supporting Ed's plan was that they do it his way.

He was sitting on the chair opposite the sofa staring at Ed and Ernesto. "You do know how dangerous this could be," he said. "Or have you forgotten about being shot at?"

Of course I do, Ed thought, I'm old, not stupid. "Bosworth asked me to let him know when I found Levi. All I have to do is get him to meet me, and you can arrest him."

"It's not that simple, Ed. I have to have probable cause. If I had enough to arrest him, I would have already done that, don't you think?"

He *hadn't* thought about that. "What if I get him to admit to something? You could put a wire on me or something. Wouldn't that work?"

Williams closed his eyes. His brow furrowed as if he'd just been struck by a massive migraine.

"Dammit, you've been watching too many cop shows on TV. Bosworth's an experienced criminal, and you're an amateur. You'd give yourself away, and he'd likely kill you on the spot without saying a word. You've been watching too many cop shows on TV. The real world doesn't work that way."

The real world, Ed thought. The word 'kill' kept echoing in his head. He felt a slight headache coming on, and was beginning to have second thoughts about his plan. But, Ed

Lazenby wasn't one to second guess himself. Even though his relationship with Williams had gotten off to an unimpressive start, the postal inspector was turning out to be a standup guy, and he seemed to know what he was doing. He hadn't been happy with what Ed proposed doing, but since he was being bullheaded about it, reluctantly went along. He'd assured Ed that this should be a quick 'in and out' operation, but it was important that Ed follow his instructions to the letter.

Ed would call Bosworth and demand a meeting to discuss Levi Crumley's location. The story Williams had suggested Ed used was that Levi was willing to come for ward and return the money he'd taken, but only with Ed as a go-between because he knew Bosworth was angry and he was afraid. If Bosworth agreed, Ed would lead him to an abandoned warehouse off Georgia Avenue near Olney, Maryland, which would be staked out by Maryland State Police, Montgomery County Police, and Postal Inspection

Service agents. He'd assured Ed that this would be the only risky part, but upon arrival, the cops would swarm Bosworth and any of his gang he happened to bring along, and all Ed had to do was duck down and stay out of the line of fire.

Pretty simple, Ed thought, at least the way Williams described it, it was simple. But, the devil's in the details. Ed tried to imagine all the things that could go wrong and end up with him getting bullet holes drilled into his body, and the things he imagined were many. It certainly didn't resemble any of the sting operations he'd seen on TV where the good buy went in with a microphone taped to his chest and got the bad guy to confess, whereupon the police came in and slapped cuffs on the bad guy and gave the good guy a medal. Williams had assured him that the plan would work without a wire; that Bosworth's acceptance of Ed's invitation was an admission of guilt of a kind—enough to justify his arrest. He spoke with such assurance, that Ed was finally convinced it just might work.

"Okay," he said. "Let's do this."

Williams smiled and stood. As Ed was putting his jacket on, Williams approached him and put his hands on both Ed's shoulders. He grabbed the collar of Ed's jacket and pulled him in until their faces were almost touching. There was a concerned look in his eyes.

"Ed, I just want you to know," he said. "I had my doubts about you at the start, but I really appreciate what you're doing. You're gonna help us put away a truly bad individual."

"So, Josh, us old codgers aren't so bad after all, eh?" Ed said.

Williams carefully adjusted and straightened the collars of Ed's jacket. "No, you're not so bad at all," he said, and patted Ed's shoulders again. "Now, let's get this show on the road."

Charles Ray

EIGHTEEN

As agreed, Ed called Bosworth. Joshua Williams stood nearby, smiling supportively.

"Ah, Mr. Lazenby," Bosworth's oily voice echoed in Ed's ear. "You have some information for me?"

"Uh, yeah, I have a lead on where Levi Crumley is."

"Good. Where is he?"

"There's a little hitch," Ed said. "He's worried you might be upset with him, and he wants me to act as a kind of go-between. I don't think you'll want to discuss it over the phone, if you know what I mean."

There was a long pause. "Uh huh, you're right about that," Bosworth said. "Okay, we'll meet up." He gave Ed an address on Georgia Avenue north of Potomac Valley

Community. "Be there in twenty minutes." The connection was abruptly broken.

Ed's hands felt sweaty.

"Everything's good so far," Williams said. "Just go to the meeting, tell him what we agreed on, and then give him the address and get the hell out of there. He might not take you along, because we're pretty sure his intent is to kill Crumley, and he might not want to have another body to dispose of."

"Huh?" Ed said.

"You know, you'd be a witness. Anyway, don't worry, we've got it covered."

Ed swallowed hard. He was suddenly wondering why he'd come up with the idea of reaching out to Bosworth in the first place. Being constantly reminded that he was dealing with a man who killed people wasn't helping his nerves.

"Hey," Williams said. "There's still time to back out of this."

"No, I'm in. I've got to get moving, I have to be at the rendezvous in less than twenty minutes."

Ed's nerves calmed during the drive; at least as far as the operation was concerned. Dealing with Washington-area drivers was always such a tension-filled situation for him it was easy to forget something as trivial as a gangster who might shoot him on sight. He kept glancing in his rearview mirrors as he drove, but saw no sign of Williams or any of the other cops, and hoped that was a sign of their skill at conducting surveillance. While he liked his solitude, this was a time he didn't want to be alone. In fact, he would have felt better with a parade of police cars surrounding him.

He'd finally convinced himself that everything would work out fine by the time he pulled into the gravel front lot of a machine shop on the west side of Georgia Avenue. The lot was empty except for a large black Buick Seville parked at the corner of the big corrugated metal building. The building appeared to be vacant. Ed pulled his 4-Runner in next to the building about twenty feet from the Buick. Taking a deep breath, he turned off the engine, opened the door and stepped out. As he walked around the rear of his vehicle, the rear door of the Buick opened and a long leg emerged, followed by a sight that caused Ed's breath to catch in his throat.

The woman emerging from the backseat of the Buick stopped Ed in his tracks. She was tall, nearly six feet, with broad shoulders and breasts that strained against the black turtle neck sweater, and a narrow waist and flaring hips that were accented by the skintight black pants encasing them. Her medium length hair was black like her costume, with streaks of gold, and it was brushed down against her skull and fell to just past her ears. An oval face with a peaches and cream complexion, full red lips, an aquiline nose, and eyes that were bright green and surrounded by lush black lashes. She brought to Ed's mind all the purple prose he'd read in the trashy paperback novels he'd bought in the Pentagon drug store years earlier, as well as the slang terms his military friends were fond of using; phrases like 'built like a brick shithouse,' and 'legs down to here,' buzzed through his brain as she approached him, her hips and breasts swaying. She was, he thought as he watched, mesmerized by her movements, what the kids called a 'hottie.' He wondered how a man like Bosworth had enticed someone like this to work for him.

They met halfway between the two vehicles. Ed was struggling to breathe normally. She stopped four feet from him, and put her hands on her hips, regarding him with her head cocked slightly to one side. Ed swallowed hard. The words 'she's the most beautiful woman I've ever seen' hardly seemed to convey what he thought. Then she smiled, and he felt his legs go rubbery.

"You're Ed Lazenby, I take it," she said in a throaty voice. "I'm Emerald. B. B. sent me to pick you up."

Of course, she'd be named Emerald with eyes that color, Ed thought, and then her words penetrated the fog in his brain—'pick you up.' "Uh, I thought he'd meet me personally," he said.

"He will," Emerald said. "Just not here. Now, if you don't mind, please lift your arms and spread your feet shoulder width apart."

Numbly, Ed complied. She ran her hands expertly over his body— every inch of his body—making him glad that Williams had nixed the idea of him wearing a wire. The sensation of her finely sculpted hands massaging his body, especially his chest and the inside of his lets was unsettling, and he hoped she wouldn't notice that she was arousing him. Finally, satisfied that he didn't have a listening device or weapon on his body, she stepped back and pointed to the Buick. "We're taking that car. I'll bring you back here for yours later."

Ed got into the back seat, and she climbed in beside him. The driver, a bull-necked black man with short peppercorn hair and a thick mustache, put the car in gear and sped out of the lot as soon as she pulled the door shut.

They drove in silence. Ed was conscious of the heat from Emerald's leg, as it occasionally touched his when the Buick took a turn. She didn't seem to be in a talkative mood, and he didn't trust himself to talk. They headed generally south, but the driver left Georgia Avenue immediately after leaving the machine shop lot, and he took so many turns, Ed had no idea where he was.

After thirty minutes, they pulled into a parking lot that surrounded a two-story gray-brick building. Beyond the parking lot on the right was an expanse of ragged grassland and beyond that a row of red brick warehouses. On the left was a large metal building with a flat roof and large steel doors that slid up and down on rollers. Several 18-wheelers without trailers were parked in front of the large building. The place was neat and well-organized, but there was no sign of work or workers, and nowhere did he see a sign identifying the establishment or its purpose.

The driver pulled in front of the center door of the gray building and stopped. Emerald got out and held the door for Ed to exit. The Buick immediately pulled away as soon as Ed got out. Emerald motioned him to follow her and they entered the building.

They entered a large space, with a waist high counter to the right and rows of plastic chairs to the left. They were the only ones there. Emerald's stiletto heels made clicking sounds on the marble floor as she led Ed toward a door in the back wall. At the door, she stopped, opened it and stood aside, motioning for Ed to enter. He stopped, looking at his guide with an expression of uncertainty.

"Go on in," she said. "B.B. doesn't like to be kept waiting."

"Ladies first," he said.

"This is a private meeting. Just B.B. and you."

He took a deep breath and stepped through the door which closed behind with a dull thump.

Once again, his breath caught in his throat. He found himself in a large office. Actually, large didn't even begin to describe it. The room he entered was huge; nearly as big as the entrance lobby of the building. From the door to the large wooden desk at the back of the room was, Ed estimated, at least fifty feet. To the left was a floor to ceiling bookcase that covered the entire wall. It was filled with leather bound books that Ed didn't need to be told were probably rare and expensive. To the right was a glass and chrome bar backed by glass shelves containing hundreds of bottles of expensive looking liquors. The floor was carpeted with an ornate Persian rug that stretched from the door to beyond the desk and from side to side. It felt like foam beneath Ed's feet, and had to have cost a small fortune.

Belmont 'B.B.' Bosworth, dressed in a shimmery blue sharkskin suit, with an ivory shirt and blood-red tie held in place by a diamond tie pin the size of a nickel, sat reclined behind the desk, eying Ed with a reptilian stare as he crossed the room.

Charles Ray

NINETEEN

Bosworth waved a manicured hand at a plush chair at the corner of the desk. "Have a seat, Ed . . . you mind if I call you Ed?" Ed shrugged. "Fine, pull up a chair, Ed. Would you care for a drink?"

Ed wasn't sure of the protocol. If a gangster offered you a drink, was it polite to refuse? Was it *safe* to do so? He decided to err on the side of caution. "Sure, do you have bourbon?"

"You name it, I got it," Bosworth said. "Any particular brand?"

"No, I'm not fussy."

Bosworth got up and walked to the bar. "You like your bourbon mixed with anything?" he asked.

"Just ice," Ed said.

"Ah, now you're a man after my own heart. Don't let nothing get between you and good Kentucky bourbon but some frozen water." Bosworth smacked his lips.

He dropped ice in two glasses and splashed a generous quantity of bourbon in each. He brought them back to the desk, handing one to Ed. Back in his plush, high-backed leather chair, he took a long pull from his glass and sighed. After wiping his lips with his fingers, he fixed Ed with a piercing gaze.

"I believe you have some information for me," he said. "Where is Levi Crumley?"

Ed took a sip of bourbon, savoring it for a moment.

"There are, ah, certain assurances Mr. Crumley insists upon before I can divulge that."

Bosworth's eyes narrowed to tiny slits. He ran his fingers over the starched cuff of his shirt and stared icily at Ed.

"We had a deal, Lazenby. You find Crumley, you tell me. You wouldn't be trying to renege now, would you?"

"You altered the terms of that

arrangement when your people shot at my friend and me."

"Oh, that." Bosworth smiled a cold and mirthless smile. "A little misunderstanding is all that was. I'm sure we can get past it."

Ed put his glass on the edge of the desk. Bosworth frowned. He got up, walked to the bar and got two ceramic coasters which he brought back. He put one under Ed's glass and the other under his own glass adjacent to the maroon desk pad in the center of his desk. Ed waited until he was seated again before speaking.

"I'm sure you can understand, though, that after what happened with us, Levi is . . . reluctant to . . . meet with you."

Bosworth waved his hand negligently. "Look, no harm, no foul," he said. "You just get old Levi on the phone and tell him all's forgiven, okay?" He took a flip phone out of the center drawer of the desk and shoved it across to Ed.

"He's willing to return your share of the money," Ed said, ignoring the phone. "He just needs your guarantee that there will be no . . . adverse action taken against him."

Bosworth had his drink halfway to his mouth. As Ed spoke, his hand froze in midair, his eyes looked as if they would pop out of their sockets, and twin circles of red blossomed on his cheeks.

"My share of the money," he said, sending a spray of spittle across the desk toward Ed. "What the fuck you mean my *share* of the money?"

"I'm just telling you what he told me." Ed stared innocently at him.

"Yeah, well lemme school you, bro." With anger, Bosworth's polished veneer peeled away and his speech dipped deeply into the patois of the streets he'd crawled up from. "*All* the fuckin' money's mine, ya hear. That scrawny, spastic little mother fucker works for *me*! He ain't nothin' but a delivery boy; he pick up the packages at The Mail Box and he deliver 'em here. We give him packages here, he deliver 'em to The Mail Box. For that, we done paid the little shit a fucking good piece of change, know what I mean. Now, he done gone and stole from me, and I can't sit here and do nothin' 'bout that, you dig. I gone set things right up in here. Got to do that if I gone maintain control. Now, where the fuck is Levi at?"

"Please now, Mr. Bosworth. Getting angry is not going to resolve this situation. I'm sure if you'll calm down you'll see that I'm right."

Bosworth pushed himself slowly up from his chair. He glared down at Ed. His eyes were bloodshot, and lines of spit dribbled from both sides of his mouth. He reached into his inside coat pocket and withdrew a pearl handled knife. Pressing a button in the side, he caused a six-inch blade to snap out with a 'snick.' He started around the desk. Ed rose, stepping back toward the door.

"Now, here how it gone be up in here, mother fucker," Bosworth said. "You gone tell me where Levi at. You gone tell me if I got to cut it out of you a word at a time, you hear what I'm sayin'? Don't think I can't do it, 'cause I done it before. That been the problem in this fucking outfit, I been delegatin' too much 'stead of doin' it myself. That how

Levi able to steal my money so long without me knowin' about it. Well, that gone change now, you bet your ass." He moved closed, waving the knife around in tight little circles in front of Ed's face. "Now, you gone start talkin', or am I gone have to start cuttin'?"

Ed couldn't take his eyes off the blade. As his eyes followed the circular motions, watching the light from the overhead fixtures glinting off the sharp steel, he understood how cobras must feel as they watch the motions of the snake charmer's musical instrument, except, in this case, the instrument contained the deadly poison, not the snake.

"Now, Mr. Bosworth," he said. "Surely we can come to some kind of arrangement."

"Ain't gone be no 'rangements," Bosworth said. "I done spent too long building this operation up to let some punk fuck with me like this. I started out just hitting marks here in the DC area, but pretty soon I was nationwide. I'm pullin' down two hundred grand a week from just that one place on Georgia Avenue, and that's after expenses. When you add in all the others, I make over a million a week, and it ain't nearly as dangerous, or as much work, as drugs or whores. All I gotta do is set there and open envelopes. Last chance before I start cuttin', old man. Where Levi at?"

Bosworth raised the knife, aiming the point of the blade at Ed's left eye. As the blade got larger and larger, all Ed could think of was, *how the hell did I get myself into this mess?*

There was the sound of something hard slamming into wood, and the sound of wood splintering.

"Drop it, Bosworth," a loud voice said.

The knife stopped its approach, and then disappeared from Ed's view.

"Down on the floor with your hands behind your head!" Ed started kneeling. "Not you, Ed." Ed recognized Joshua Williams' voice. "Bosworth, you keep your hands where I can see them. Officer, cuff that piece of shit."

His legs got rubbery and he sank to his knees anyway. Williams helped him up. As he looked around, he saw Bosworth face down with his hands behind his back, a uniformed police officer snapping handcuffs on his wrists, and he wasn't being too gentle about it. Bosworth had craned his head up and was glaring at Ed with angry, bloodshot eyes.

"You sneaky old fuck, you done set me up," shouted. "I shoulda cut your ass when you first come in."

"Shut up, Bosworth," Williams said. "You're under arrest, and you have the right to remain silent. Unless you want me to kick you in the face, you'll exercise that right."

He made a menacing move toward the gangster who was being hauled roughly to his feet by the uniformed officer.

"You can't do that," Bosworth said. "I know my rights. That be police brutality."

Williams growled. "Get this asshole out of here, officer," he said. He turned back to Ed.

"You okay, Ed?"

"Y-yeah, I'm okay. H-how'd you find me?" Ed asked.

Williams reached up and flipped

up first his right and then his left collar. Straining to look down, Ed saw two button-like objects affixed to the underside of his collar.

"I put these on you just before you left the house," Williams said. "One's a locator beacon. It sends a signal to a satellite that enabled us to track you. The other's a very sensitive microphone/transmitter. With that, we got Bosworth's confession recorded all nice and neat."

Ed frowned at him. "Why d- didn't you tell me you were planting these things on me? And, why did you think they'd be necessary?"

"Hope for the best, plan for the worst is my philosophy," Williams said. "I didn't tell you so there'd be no risk of you accidentally giving them away, and I figured they'd do what they did. Bosworth would want you on home turf. I also knew that you'd get him talking. You have that way about you. Worked like a charm, too. We got enough in his own words to put him away for a long, long time. Oh, and don't worry. I had an agent pick your car up. It's back at your house."

Ed let out a breath. "I must say, you had a brilliant plan. I just wish I'd been let in on it. I should be upset with you, but the way you did it was probably best. I just wish you hadn't cut it so close. I almost wet my pants there when he came at me with that knife."

"Oh, that's just icing on the cake. Attempted murder will be added to the charges against him."

As Ed and Williams started to follow the officers who were hauling Bosworth out, Ed put his hand on the younger man's shoulder. "What about Levi Crumley? Are you still interested in him?"

Williams smiled. "Only as a material witness based on what Bosworth said. I don't think the U.S. Attorney will be interested in prosecuting someone like him. He'll have his hands full dealing with Bosworth and his main goons . . . and goonettes—that was some escort you had. When you find him have him give me a call."

"What about the clerk at The Mail Box?" Ed asked.

"I had the county cops go there to arrest him, but he must have suspected something was going down. He's in the wind. No matter, though, as long as we have the big fish." He regarded him for a few seconds. "I want to thank you for what you did. Took a lot of guts to do what you did, and it was an honor working with you. If you ever tell anyone I said that, though, I'll deny the hell out of it."

"Pleasure working with you too, Josh," Ed said. "And, I will also deny I ever said it."

Charles Ray

TWENTY

Williams gave Ed a lift back to his house, where they found Ernesto waiting with a worried look on his face.

"I'm fine," Ed said. "Got a little exciting right at the end, but Josh here came in just in the nick of time and arrested the bad guys."

"Dammit, Ed," Ernesto said. "You get to have all the fun."

Williams made a wry face. "You have a strange concept of what's fun. What he did was dangerous, and I'm just glad it worked out okay. Look, again, I want to thank you guys for your help, but frankly, I hope we don't run into each other again." He reached for Ed's collar and removed the tracking and monitoring devices and put them in his own jacket pocket.

"Aw, come on," Ernesto said. "Why don't admit it. You enjoyed working with us."

"Yeah, about as much as a root canal. You two better stay out of trouble . . . hell, what am I saying, you guys will be up to something before I'm out of sight."

They shook hands all around and Williams, after clapping both of them on the shoulders, left them standing there in Ed's living room.

"Did you find Abigail's grandson?" Ernesto asked.

Ed removed his jacket and put it in the closet near the entrance. "No, but I think I know where he is."

"So, what next?"

"First, I'm going to make a pot of coffee and a sandwich. You want one?"

"You ever know me to turn down food . . . unless you're having something with no meat that is."

"No, I was thinking of ham sandwiches," Ed said. "With some of that store-bought potato salad I picked up at Giant."

"Well, what're we waiting for," Ernesto said, heading for the kitchen.

Two hours later they were in Ed's 4-Runner sitting in the parking lot two shops down from The Mail Box. Except for the single bulb over the entrance, the place looked dark and empty.

"Doesn't look like anyone's in there," Ernesto said.

"That's what I'm banking on," Ed said. "Come on, let's go."

Looking puzzled, Ernesto followed him after they got out of the vehicle. Ed walked along the sidewalk, past The Mail Box until they came to a gap between shops, an alley leading around bchind thc buildings. Ed turned left and walked until they came to a building with a sign over a fragile looking wooden door that read,

'The Mail Box – Deliveries.'

"Well," he said. "Here we are."

Ernesto continued to look puzzled. Ed grasped the door handle and twisted. It turned and the door swung outward.

"Wha—" Ernesto's mouth popped open.

"I figured it wouldn't be locked," Ed said. Quietly he eased inside with Ernesto crowding in behind him.

They found themselves in a small dark room crammed with stacks of packing boxes. Ed turned and opened the door to allow some light in. He saw a cord hanging from a ceiling fixture. He reached up and pulled it. A single low-wattage bulb illuminated. He closed the door.

"What now?" Ernesto whispered.

Ed sniffed the air. Sure enough, there was that wet dog smell, stronger in the stuffy room than it had been in the shop outside.

He hadn't made the connection at first. The outer area of The Mail Box held a variety of odors; the stale tobacco and sweaty smell of Pimply face, the mustiness of packing boxes, and that faint odor of wet dog. It had nagged at Ed's consciousness, that sensation of something familiar just at the edge of awareness. And, then, in a flash it had come to him. It was actually quite smart; something the average person might not have thought of.

He inspected the space, trying to put himself in the position of someone who might want to conceal himself, but who would want to leave a way out should it be necessary to make a quick getaway. Starting with the ceiling, he eyeballed it carefully starting in the corner left of the door and working in a zig-zag pattern to the wall opposite the door. The wallboard panels that made up the ceiling didn't look disturbed, nor did he see any indication of a trapdoor or other access to the crawlspace beneath the building's roof beyond the small square through which the heating, water, and electrical lines were routed. The boxes were stacked to either side of the door, broken on the left by space for the door into the main business area at the front of the building. The stacks were one box deep of square 14 by 14 inch boxes. They were all lined up, but for the last two boxes on the right side, which protruded nearly 12 inches beyond the rest. He walked toward the protruding boxes, sniffing the air as he did. The rank odor of wet animal hair was so thick he almost felt like gagging. In combination with all the other smells in such a tight space, it had his eyes watering.

Ernesto tagged along behind him, wrinkling his nose at the odor and watching in wonder. At the pushed-out boxes Ed stopped. The odor was particularly strong here and definitely coming from behind the boxes.

"I think Levi Crumley is somewhere in the vicinity," Ed said.

"Oh yeah, where?" Ernesto asked.

There was a scuffling sound. Ernesto opened his mouth to speak, but Ed silenced him by putting a hand over his mouth.

"I don't know, but if I could find him, I'd tell him that that gangster, Bosworth, has been arrested, and that the cops don't want to arrest him because they know he was forced to do what he did." He aimed his voice not at Ernesto but down at the boxes.

"Wha—" Ed put a finger to his own lips, silencing his friend again.

"They want Levi to testify about

the fraud operation, and in exchange for his testimony he'll be left alone," Ed spoke toward the boxes again. "He's no longer in any trouble."

The scuffling sound became louder. One of the boxes inched toward Ed's foot. Ernesto's eyes went round and he stepped back until he bumped into the stack of boxes on the opposite wall.

"What the hell!"

"Probably just rats," Ed said. "I hear they get pretty big and mean around here."

Along with the scuffling, there was a low moaning sound.

"Damn," Ernesto said. "It'd have to be a big sucker to move that box."

"Yeah, they can bite your finger off, and you don't even want to see what they can do to a person's face."

There was a squealing sound, and the box shot forward, followed by a pair of dirty sneakers below frayed jeans.

"Ng-g-gh! Help," a squeaky voice said.

A small figure cringed against the wall, slapping at his jeans and a

Charles Ray

dirty gray sweater.

"Levi Crumley, I presume," Ed said as he grabbed the small man by the shoulders.

"Lemme go, I d-didn't do n-nothin'," Crumley cried. "I wanna g-go home." Tears streamed down his smudged cheeks and as he talked the smell of his breath almost made Ed gag.

Ed gripped his shoulders harder and shook him.

"Look at me, Levi!" he commanded. "No one's going to hurt you. We're friends of your grandma, Abigail, here to take you home."

Crumley's body stopped shaking, but the tears still flowed freely over his cheeks. He looked up at Ed, having to crane his head back to do so. "Y-you know g-gramma?"

"Yes, she's a friend of ours," Ed said. "She asked us to find you and bring you home."

"And, you not t-takin' me to jail?"

"No, Levi, we're not taking you to jail. Like I said, the police just want you to tell them the things Bosworth made you do. You'll be a hero if you do that."

A shy smile crept onto the grimy face. "H-hero, I'll be a hero? I like that. C-can I tell gramma?"

"Sure, you can tell her. Are you ready to go home? You need to wash up before you go and talk to the police."

"Okay, but I'm hungry. C-can we g-get some hamburgers?"

Ernesto eased up and put his mouth close to Ed's ear. "You want this kid to ride in the car with us?" he whispered. "It'll take a week to wash the stink out."

Ed frowned at him and turned back to Crumley. "Sure we can get hamburgers." He put a hand on the kid's shoulder. "Come on, let's go."

Crumley looked around. "You not gonna let the rats get me, right? I don't like rats. They stink."

Even Ernesto had to laugh at that.

Charles Ray

TWENTY-ONE

They wound up driving to a nearby Burger King and Levi hadn't been kidding when he said he wanted 'hamburgers.' Ed ended up buying two Whoppers, a large order of fries and a large strawberry shake, which the kid started eating before they could get to a corner table, dropping crumbs and, burning his tongue in the process, but cooling it off with the shake. Afterwards they drove him to Abigail's house.

When she answered the door, she grabbed the kid's collar and dragged him into the living room. She alternated between cuffing his ears and hugging him, apparently oblivious to the rank smell emanating from his body.

"Boy, where have you been? I was worried sick about you," she said.

"I'm okay, gramma. I was at the shop. Nobody knew I was there, but Mr. Ed here, him and his friend found me."

"What on earth were you doing there, Levi? What if that man Bosworth had found you?"

"Aw, gramma, Mr. Bosworth, he don't never come to the shop, and Pete, the guy that runs it, never come into the back room hardly, except to smoke, and he never paid attention. I just sat there behind the boxes and stayed real quiet."

She hugged him. "I'm just glad you're okay."

"I hate to interrupt a family reunion, Abigail," Ed said. "But, Levi needs to get cleaned up so we can go talk to Inspector Williams."

She stepped back and looked wide-eyed at Ed. "But, he can't go to jail. You see how he is; he'd never survive in jail."

"Don't worry, he won't go to jail. I have Williams' word on it. They just want a statement from him to use against Bosworth."

"Really?"

"Really," Ernesto said. "I was there when he told Ed that. Levi's got nothing to worry about. All he has to do is give his statement."

"He might not even have to testify at the trial," Ed said.

She let out a breath. "Okay then," she said. "Levi, you go get yourself washed up and put on some clean clothes. And, don't you forget to clean good behind your ears, and . . . every place else, you hear." Smiling and bobbing his head, the kid skipped off toward the bathroom. She looked at him with a motherly expression on her face. For once, she looked almost human. When he disappeared behind the bathroom door, she turned back to Ed. "I owe you some money, Ed, wait here and I'll go get it." She scurried off to her bedroom.

Three minutes later she came back. She handed Ed a thick wad of twenty dollar bills. "You can count it if you want to," she said. "That's five thousand dollars. I'd give you more if I had it."

"Not necessary, Abigail," Ed

said. He stuffed the cash into his jacket pocket. "Ernesto and I are going to my place and change. Call us when Levi's cleaned up and we'll come get him and take him to see Williams."

She reached out and grasped Ed's bicep. "Thank you for bringing my boy home. Thank you both. He's all the family I got left. I don't know what I'd have done if something had happened to him."

The session with Postal Inspector Joshua Williams went better than Ed had expected it would. Once Williams saw the level of Levi Crumley's emotional development, he was convinced that the kid had been a more or less unwitting dupe of Belmont Bosworth. He walked him through a statement of the things Bosworth had made him do, had him sign it in his childish scrawl, and they took him home.

Over the next couple of weeks, things happened in dribs and drabs, filtered to Ed and Ernesto through various methods, ranging from radio announcements or newspaper stories to gossip overheard in the community center.

The news that had both of them cheering and high-fiving around Ed's living room was an announcement on the local NPR station that Belmont 'B.B.' Bosworth, notorious DC crime boss, was being indicted by the United Stated Attorney for the District of Columbia on multiple counts of mail fraud and identity fraud. In addition, because he was the head of a criminal enterprise, he was being indicted under the 1970 RICO Act, which allows for extended penalties for the heads of organizations involved in racketeering, and allows them to be prosecuted for ordering subordinates to perform illegal acts. The announcer said that Bosworth was suspected of involvement in other criminal activity, but the government didn't have ironclad evidence to support indictments. Not that it mattered, because the charges for which he was being indicted were supported by strong evidence in the form of a taped confession from Bosworth himself, obtained through the assistance of a local citizen whose name was being withheld for privacy and security reasons.

One piece of news, obtained first from overhearing an idle comment in the main room of the community center, and then verified with their own eyes, was met with mixed emotions. The overheard news was that the Wicked Witch of PVC was moving out. Ed and Ernesto went immediately to Abigail's house where they found a moving van parked partially on the sidewalk, and two muscular Hispanic men in green and yellow overalls trundling packing boxes on little trolleys from the house to the van.

They entered through the front door, which was held open by a small red plastic step stool, to find Abigail Crumley standing in the middle of a now-empty living room watching the moving men with a stern look on her face. The stern look softened a degree or two when she saw Ed and Ernesto.

"Uh, hello," she said. "What're you two doing here?"

Ernesto looked around. "Just dropped by to see if the rumors about you moving were true."

She laughed. "You mean the ones about the Wicked Witch of PVC going back to the Land of Oz." At their shocked looks she continued, "Oh, I've heard all that talk that was supposed to be behind my back."

"Never heard the one about the Land of Oz," Ernesto said.

They both laughed.

"Why are you moving?" Ed asked.

Her left eyebrow arched upwards, like the Leonard Nimoy character in the 'Star Trek' stories. "After all that's happened, I thought Levi needed a new environment. Besides, I'm tired of the cold weather here, so we're moving to Florida."

"Isn't that expensive?"

"No more so than living up here," she said. "Besides, I found a good deal down in St. Petersburg. They have a school there for people like Levi. It'll help him learn to . . . take care of himself. I won't be around forever, you know."

"Oh, I think you'll outlive us all," Ed said. "Anyway, I wish you the best. You'll be missed here at PVC."

She made a snorting sound.

"Oh, these old biddies will find someone else to be the villain soon enough." She gave Ernesto a lingering look. "Will *you* miss me?"

Ernesto swallowed hard, and Ed clamped his lips tight to keep from laughing.

"W-why, of course I'll miss you," Ernesto said. "Ed and I both will."

"When we get settled, I'll send you the address," she said. "Maybe you can come visit me."

"Uh, yeah, maybe."

The silence stretched out until it was becoming awkward.

"Well," Ed said. "We just came to say goodbye, we'll get out of your way. Tell Levi goodbye for us."

There didn't seem to be anything else to say after that, so they shook hands. Ed thought Abigail's handshake, though firm, was a bit shaky, and even though she had a tiny hint of a smile on her face, she wouldn't meet his gaze.

"Goodbye, Abigail," Ed said. "You take care of yourself, and take good care of Levi."

"I will, Ed. I always have."

TWENTY-TWO

Monday, February 2, was a cloudy, gloomy day. It also happened to be Groundhog Day. Ed and Ernesto sat in the dining room in the community center of Potomac Valley Community, at the 'undesirable' table in the corner near the window. There seemed to be an extra chill in the air, and through the window all they could see was gray. It was 7:15 in the morning, and the bulk of the breakfast crowd had yet to arrive. In fact, the skinny attendant, her hair covered by a white lace hairnet, was the only other person there.

"I reckon the groundhog ain't gonna get scared by his shadow today," Ernesto said.

Ed looked out the window. "Hell, he probably won't even bother coming out at all with gloomy weather like this. If I'd been smart, I would have stayed at home and cooked breakfast."

"But, the bad weather . . . that's a good thing, right? I mean, that means winter's almost over."

Ed laughed. "You really buy that? You know that groundhogs only come out this time of year because they're waking up from hibernation and they come out of their burrows looking for food and mates."

"So, they're hungry *and* horny. Seems to me they wouldn't be scared of a shadow under those conditions. Still, you know the saying, no shadow, no more winter."

"You know, amigo," Ed said. "I've always been confused about something. How is it, that in a country where so many people, politicians included, refuse to believe in global warming, you have so many who are willing to believe a silly superstition

about a furry rodent's ability to pre-
dict the weather?"

Ernesto shrugged and shoveled
more food in his mouth. "Everyone's
gotta believe in something," he
mumbled around a mouthful of
scrambled eggs.

"How about the Tooth Fairy or
the Easter Bunny," Ed said. "At
least they leave something behind
you can use."

"Hey, I believe in them too," Ernesto protested. "Speaking of things
that are hard to believe, what about
Abigail picking up and moving like
that? What do you think that was
that all about?"

"Maybe she just wanted to get
Levi away from the memories of
what happened here," Ed said, looking down at his plate and playing
with his food.

Ernesto stopped eating. "Yeah,
right. Look, amigo, I been hanging
around you long enough I've started
to be able to tell when someone's
bullshitting me. You don't believe
that for a minute."

Ed put his fork down and fixed
his friend with a piercing stare.

"You're right, of course," he said. "I don't believe that's why she moved."

"Then, spill it, man. Why did she move?"

Ed leaned forward, lowering his voice, "Okay, I have a theory. I'll share it with you, but you have to promise not to breathe a word of to another living soul."

Ernesto made the sign of the cross over his left breast. "Scout's honor, I'll never tell. So, spill. Why'd she move?"

"Did you take a good look at the money Abigail gave me; the money I shared with you?"

"Nah, I just put it in my . . . piggy bank," Ernesto said. "By the way, thanks for sharing fifty-fifty. You didn't have to do that."

"You didn't notice anything strange about that money?"

"Strange, strange in what way?" He rubbed at his chin, and his brow furrowed in concentration. His eyes went wide. "It's not counterfeit, is it?" He got a worried look on his face.

Ed shook his head.

"They were all twenties, Ernesto, every last one of 'em. Didn't you notice that?"

"O-o-okay, so she gave us a bunch of twenty dollar bills, so what's the big deal about that?"

Ed put his elbows on the table and rested his forehead against his palms. He heaved a heavy sigh.

"*What!*" Ernesto said plaintively.

"Haven't you been paying attention the past couple of weeks? What was Levi Crumley transporting for that gangster?"

"Uh, boxes with envelopes full of—" His face lit up. He smiled and smacked his forehead with his palm. "Ri-i-ight, envelopes from people who fell for his mail scam. Envelopes with money in them, twenty dollar bills to be exact."

"Finally." Ed shook his head again. "That's right. Now, it doesn't prove anything beyond a shadow of a doubt, but who has that much money, and all in the same denomination?"

"Whoa! You saying she paid us with some of the money Levi skimmed from his gangster boss? Uh, we're not gonna have to turn it in, are we?"

Ed shook his head. "No, I'm not saying it's money *Levi* skimmed, and since we don't have any proof, I see no need to even mention it to anyone, much less turn it in."

Actually, he *had* very briefly considered turning it in, but after reflecting on the mess it would cause, decided to keep it.

"Now, you got me confused, compadre." Ernesto's brow wrinkled in concentration. "If it's not the money from the scam, where did it come from?"

"I didn't say it wasn't money from the scam, I'm saying I don't think Levi was the one who took it."

"Wha-, how? If it's money from the scam, who else but Levi could have taken it?"

"Ernesto, you saw that kid," Ed said. "He can't even brush his teeth without instructions. Sure, that was pretty slick, the way he hid out from that gang right under their noses, but that was nothing more than animal instinct—he hid in a place that was familiar to him. There's no way he'd come up with the idea of skimming money, or even looking in those envelopes, on his own."

"So, someone put him up to it. But, who would . . . whoa, you're not saying you think Abigail was the—"

Ed held up a hand. "I'm not saying anything. And, neither are you. She's all that kid's got, and I think the two of them have been through enough already. I was just pointing out the obvious."

"But, if she's capable of trying to skim a gangster, what's it gonna be like down there in Florida with a town full of retired senior citizens? Hell, with a whole state full of retirees."

"They'll have to look out for themselves," Ed said. "Wouldn't you agree?"

"Yeah, I reckon you're right," Ernesto said, smiling broadly. "They got the good weather, let 'em pay for it."

Just then, the door to the dining room swung open as if pushed by a strong breeze, and in fact, two— strike that—one force of nature, breezed through. Violet Wertheim, her flame-red hair piled atop her head, her cheeks scarlet from the cold, wrapped in a fake fur stole, came through the door like the leading wave of a hurricane. Her sister, Rose, her close-cropped gray-streaked blue hair flapping weakly as she bobbed along, with her chin tucked into the collar of her dark blue wool coat, followed meekly in her wake, like leaves pulled along in the wake of a strong wind.

Violet spotted Ed and Ernesto, and, without breaking stride, veered in their direction, pulling Rose along.

"So," Violet's voice boomed across the room. "There you two are. We stopped at your house, Ed Lazenby. Rang the bell for the longest time, and no one answered. Then, dear sweet Rose here figured you'd be here eating breakfast. Actually, figured the both of you'd be here. Mind if we join you?"

Without waiting for agreement, she sat to Ed's right. Rose smiled wanly and nodded weakly at them, but took the empty seat next to Ernesto. Her smile became broader and brighter as she looked at him.

"Of course, we're happy to have you join us," Ed said. "How was your vacation, when did you get back?"

"Violet insisted we take the red-eye flight," Rose said. "We flew all night, and then when we got out of the taxi an hour ago, she insisted we come to breakfast. Actually, she insisted we first go invite you and Ernesto to breakfast."

"Now, Rose," Violet said. "You're mistaken. It was you who suggested we invite Ernesto and Ed to join us for breakfast, after I pointed out that we needed to eat something because that dreck they call food on the airplane was inedible."

Rose blinked. "Oh, yes, I guess you're right. I forgot. I haven't slept in over twelve hours."

"You must be exhausted," Ernesto said. He laid a hand on hers, causing her to blush deeply.

"Oh, Rose, stop being such a crybaby," Violet said. She snapped her fingers at the dining room attendant. "Gertrude, over here, we'd like to order breakfast."

The woman came over, frowning down at her. "My name's Norma, ma'am, not Gertrude," she said.

"And, I can serve you coffee and juice, but you should get your food from the buffet."

"Nonsense, we pay enough to this place to justify getting better service," Violet said. "Now, my sister and I'll have eggs over easy, one each, a slice of bacon, and two slices of whole wheat toast . . . and, some orange marmalade. Now, chop-chop; we've been on a plane all night, and I'm famished. Can't eat that terrible airline food, you know."

The woman looked from Ed to Ernesto. They merely shrugged and looked down at their plates. Rose closed her eyes as if by doing so she could make the whole scene go away. Finally, the woman shrugged and walked away. Ed didn't doubt that she'd be back with the food as Violet had ordered. Violet Wertheim had a way of getting exactly what she wanted, without regard to whose feelings were trampled in the process, which was one of the reasons she'd been kidnapped the previous year. Despite her acerbic personality, though, Ed liked her—sort of—and, she and her sister were among his and Ernesto's closest friends in the community.

"It's good to have you back, Violet; you too, Rose," he said. "The community's just not the same without the two of you around."

"Well, of course not," Violet said. "I imagine it was as boring as watching paint dry while we were gone."

Ed and Ernesto shared a look and a half-smile.

"Yep, you're right," Ed said. "While you were gone, absolutely nothing happened."

Charles Ray

Coriolis Effect
BUTTERFLY EFFECT

Introducing Ed Lazenby and his best friend, Ernesto Cardoza. Two residents of Potomac Valley Community, where life is anything but retiring.

ONE

"Pass the salt," the red-haired woman said. She stared across the table, a glint in her icy blue eyes, as if daring her dining companions to point out her lack of courtesy. Waiting for a response, she played with a bouncy tendril of hair that hung over her left ear.

Ed Lazenby ran a medium brown left hand slowly through his close-cropped black hair, almost able to feel the gray that streaked through the waves that resulted from the vigorous brushing he'd given it that morning. His expression was neutral. He was accustomed to Violet Wertheim's bluntness and lack of manners, so he ignored her, looking instead at the pork chops and home fried potatoes on his plate.

213

Their two dining companions, Violet's sister, Rose, and Ed's best friend, Ernesto Cardoza, sat in quiet tension, waiting for Ed to point out Violet's failure to use the magic word 'please,' which would be required before he passed her the salt which was near his right hand, and too far away for her to reach. Neither of them would even dare reach across Ed to do it. He was known to be adamant on such things. No courtesy, no service.

Moments passed. Everyone maintained stony expressions, except Violet, whose cheeks bloomed pink against her pale face. She tapped one of her long, bright red fingernails against the bowl of soup in front of her, making a clicking sound.

"It would really be nice if I could get the salt," she said. There was a tinge of stridency in her voice.

Ed looked across the table at her, following up with a stoic gaze at Rose on his right, and then Ernesto on his left. Violet returned his gaze with a semi-glare, but the other two found the bowls of soup sitting in front of them more interesting. It

had been that way for the three
years he'd been a resident of Potomac Valley Community, a collection
of small cottages and apartment
units for people aged 65 and over,
known as PVC to all the residents.
Located on the east side of Norbeck
Road, four miles north of Georgia
Avenue, it was one of several retirement communities in the area.
While most people just called it PVC
because of the tendency in the
Washington, DC area to reduce everything to initials, many of the residents, Ed included, likened it to the
sewer pipes made of the same material. The houses were small, but had
more space than the condos, and he
liked having a lawn. Laid out in a
grid pattern with interconnecting
winding paths, the streets had
names like Wisteria, Cypress, Palm,
and Maple. Most of the trees on the
main part of the grounds, though,
were oak and birch, with a few evergreens. There was also an 18-hole
golf course, six tennis courts, shuf-
fle board courts, and several small
buildings used for art lessons, pot-
tery, and several other activities that

residents were encouraged to partic-
ipate in. Across Norbeck was a row
of small, modest single story homes
owned by people who'd lived in the
area long before the retirement
communities went up, and behind
PVC was a large, undeveloped forest
park where deer, squirrels, and other wildlife romped in profusion,
since no hunting was allowed in the
vicinity of the community.

He'd moved there two days after
his birthday, a day after his retirement from his job as a systems analyst for the Department of Defense.
He'd met, Ernesto, a retired postal
worker, the first day. Like him, Ernesto was 68, and, both being widow-
ers, had hit it off immediately. The
Wertheim sisters, Violet, age 70, and
Rose, age 66, had been a part of
their foursome for only eighteen
months, and despite the continual
standoff between Ed and Violet over
courtesy, they were the closest of
friends. Violet and Rose had never
been married, a fact that Ed had
concluded was what led to Violet's
abrasive personality. He could never
figure out why the younger
Wertheim sister was so sweet na-

tured—probably a defense mechanism to enable her to get along with her more abrasive older sibling. When Violet got off on one of her tirades, usually having to do with the poor quality of the food served in the dining room of PVC's large community center, Rose would just play with her short hair, which on this particular evening had been dyed bright blue.

Finally, as he'd known would happen, he took a deep breath and focused his brown eyes on Violet.

"You know, Vi," he said, making an effort to keep the frustration he felt out of his voice. "It would be nice if you'd say please once in a while."

Violet made a snorting sound, which was easy to do given her large nose that to Ed resembled a pink banana that had been cut off near the end. That was another difference between the sisters. Rose's nose was small and narrow, straight from bridge to the end.

"Aw, give it a rest, Ed," she said. "What's such a big deal about one little word? You'd think the world will come to an end if I don't say

please when I ask you to do something."

"Well now, Violet my dear, it
might seem a small thing to you,
but to the person on the receiving
end, it just might be the biggest
thing to happen to him or her all
day." He paused and looked at her,
his left eyebrow arched. "Now, do
you still want that salt?"

She rolled her eyes. "Small
things, small things; I'll bet you're
one of those people who believe a
butterfly flapping its wings in the
Amazon can cause a hurricane in
Texas."

Ed shrugged.

"I don't know about that," he
said. "But, I do know that a small
change in one state of a determinis-
tic nonlinear system can result in
large differences in a later state.
That's a part of chaos theory. It's
like when you throw dice. Small
changes in the trajectory, the force
exerted, the angle at which you hold
your hand, can have an impact on
what numbers turn up. That's why
it's impossible to throw dice twice
exactly the same way. Edward Lo-
renz came up with the name butter-

fly theory for the phenomenon, although when he first studied it, the example was a seagull flapping its wings."

Violet rolled her eyes and snorted again.

"Do you really believe that crap? I mean, seriously, a seagull's wings?"

"I'm no meteorologist, so I don't know diddly about the weather or birds either for that matter. But, when I did systems analysis at the Defense Department, I saw for myself how tiny little maladjustments could sometimes screw up an entire system. Like a GI failing to make sure a key screw on a tank tread was properly tightened, causing the tread to loosen during a maneuver, throwing off a whole plan because a key tank couldn't get where it was needed, when it was needed. So, yeah, Vi, I do believe that crap. It's for real."

Ernesto slapped his brown hand on the table, causing the dishes to rattle.

"That's for sure," he said. "When I was delivering mail one time, I stopped for a little mid-morning snack. Bought myself a hot dog, but didn't have time to eat it all, so I rolled it up in the napkin and put it on the dash of my mail van. I'd plumb forgot about it until about an hour later, I was just about to get out and put mail in this apartment's mailboxes, when this big damn Doberman came roaring out of a vacant lot beside the building." He paused and took a sip of soup, smacking in satisfaction. "Anyway, there I was, my hands full of mail and the door wide open, and this big dog coming at me full tilt. I backed up into the van, and as I was doing so, I accidentally knocked that damned leftover hotdog out onto the sidewalk. Dog screeched to a full stop and ignored me as he wolfed that hotdog down. Gave me time to get in the van and close the door and get the hell out of there."

Rose Wertheim bobbed her head up and down. Her blue-dyed hair cut short, hanging just over the tops of her ears waving with the motion.

"I agree. You remember, Violet, that time you found Uncle Mortimer's spectacles for him. Just a small thing, but he was so im-

pressed, when he died, he left everything to you."

Violet laid a bony finger against
the side of her prominent nose,
smiling wistfully. With her free hand
she caught the end of one of her
scarlet curls and twisted it.

"Yes, I do remember that," she
said. "It was the only thing I ever did
for the old coot, but he thought it
was the nicest thing anyone had ever done for him. Truth is, it probably
was." She looked at Ed and then
Ernesto. "You have to understand . .
. our Uncle Mortimer was a real
turd."

"Violet, watch your language. Ladies don't talk like that," Rose said.

"Oh, pshaw, Rose, stop being
such a goody two shoes."

Rose's cheeks reddened.

"I am *not* a goody two shoes," she
protested. "I just don't believe in using filthy language."

"Why is it you never say anything
to Ed or Ernesto? These two repro-
bates curse like sailors sometimes."

Rose's cheeks got darker, and
she looked at Ernesto from beneath
lowered lids.

"Oh, they don't curse all that much," she said. "Besides, it's different for men."

Violet laughed a hoarse, deep throated laugh that caused Ed to cringe—hopefully not so much that she'd notice.

"Rose, darling," she said. "If it's okay for a man to say something, it should be okay for a woman, or have you decided to turn in your women's lib pin?"

"Of course not . . . it's just . . . oh, never mind, go ahead and be as foul-mouthed as you want to be."

Janet Murphy, a short blonde with small breasts and wide hips, wearing a pair of brown pants that reached to the middle of her thin calves but stretched across her hips, had been standing nearby watching the four old friends banter. With a smile on her pixie-like face she walked up to the table, standing behind Violet.

"Aren't you guys going to finish your soup, so you can try the special main course I've prepared for tonight?"

Murphy was the dietician for PVC. She had been for eight years. A thirty-one year old native of nearby Rockville, Maryland, she'd started out as an assistant to the dietician, taking over the job two years later, upon her boss's retirement. While her cooking sometimes left something to be desired, it was at least palatable most of the time, and Ed liked the fact that she always had a smile on her face, and she was unfailingly polite to everyone.

"What is tonight's special, Janet?" Ed asked.

"We're having surf and turf," she said. "I received a shipment of lobsters, and am serving them with filet mignon and baby carrots."

"I hope the steak's tender this time," Violet said. "Last time, I almost broke a tooth trying to chew it."

Murphy's face flushed dark crimson, her mouth opening and closing, and tears welling up in the corner of her eyes. She fiddled with the top button of her white blouse.

"Violet Anne Wertheim," Rose said. "You should be ashamed of yourself. You're making this sweet young thing cry."

"Yeah, Violet," Ernesto said, laying a hand on Rose's arm as he spoke, causing her cheeks to go red. "That's not nice, not nice at all."

Violet shot Ed an imploring look, her brows raised.

"What they said," he said simply. Not that he disagreed with her. The steaks in question had been so tough; he'd taken so long to eat even half of one; he'd passed on dessert.

Violet shrugged and pursed her lips, looking like a student who's just been chastised by the principal.

"Oh, all right." She turned and looked up at Murphy. "I'm sorry, dear. I was just being cranky, you know. Comes with being old, I guess. The steak was really unique, and I'm sure tonight's steak will be just the same."

There wasn't an iota of sincerity in her voice, and Ed noticed that she hadn't said the steak tasted good. But, Janet Murphy didn't seem to notice, or if she did, didn't seem to care. She beamed proudly.

"Why thank you, Violet," she said. "I'll prepare a plate especially for you . . . some extra carrots, and you get an extra helping of dessert.

We're having chocolate mousse to-night."

"You can keep the extra carrots, dear, but I do like the idea of an extra helping of dessert."

Murphy was still smiling when she turned away.

"Hey, Violet," Ed said. "Your soup's getting cold."

"But, it's not salty enough," she said.

Ed cocked his head to one side and looked down at the salt shaker.

"Oh, all right," she said, blowing a gust of air through her lips. "Ed, would you pass the salt, please?"

He picked the shaker up and bowed his head as he passed it across to her.

"Most happy to oblige, my dear," he said. "Now, that wasn't so bad was it?"

She ignored him for a few seconds as she sprinkled an unhealthy amount of salt into her soup. Then she dipped her spoon into the cream of spinach soup and stirred until the layer of salt crystals floating on the surface was pulled under. She filled the spoon and made slurping noises as she ate it.

"Hmm, now that's good." She looked at Ed. "It was . . . oh, how can I put this? It was at least better than getting a colonoscopy."

Two

The steak actually turned out to be edible—a bit tough, but edible—and the lobster was, in Violet's words, divine, which coming from her was high praise. She passed on the carrots, and had a second helping of dessert. The four of them had coffee after dinner, played a few hands of bridge, and then retired to their separate residences, three small cottages in the same block of Wisteria Lane, after agreeing to meet the following day, Saturday at 7:30, for brunch and coffee in the community's center.

As friends often tend to do, the four of them shared common tastes, often selecting, without consultation, the same dishes when they dined together. This Saturday was no different. They each took scrambled eggs, ham, toast, coffee, and orange juice. After the first forkful of scrambled eggs, Violet made a face as if she'd just bitten into an unripe persimmon.

"Oh, my goodness," she said. "Eating these eggs is like chewing on cotton wool."

Ed looked around. Janet Murphy stood near the heavily laden buffet table, smiling over each resident who passed by. He was concerned that she might hear Violet's critique. Not that it was unjustified—his first mouthful of eggs was like biting down on cardboard—but, he felt that Murphy tried her best, and it wasn't fair to constantly pick at her over her shortcomings. It would be nice if PVC had a cook who could actually . . . cook, but he wasn't sure there was anything the residents could do about other than cook their own meals—something he avoided as often as possible. What Ed did know was that if encouraged, Violet could go on for hours, and the more she talked, the more strident and insulting she often became. Even though he had to wash each forkful down with a large swallow of

either coffee or orange juice, he sol-
diered on, ignoring Violet's outburst.
Rose and Ernesto were accustomed
to following Ed's lead. Neither of
them relished being on the receiving
end of Violet's outbursts, so they
just shoved the scrambled eggs
aside and focused on the other
items on their plates.

Violet wasn't stupid. She knew
when she was being willfully ignored.

"*Well*, am I right or not? Are
these not the absolute worse eggs
you're ever eaten."

She was getting louder. Ed wanted to divert her; in the first instance
to spare Murphy's feelings, and in
the second, because he and Ernesto
had a round of golf scheduled for
immediately after the meal and he
didn't want the mental distraction
screwing up his already way-too-
much over par game.

"Actually, Violet," he said quietly.
"They're *not* the worse, not by a long
shot. When I was in the army, we
sometimes got powdered eggs in the
mess hall."

In that he was telling the truth.
In some of the facilities he'd been

forced to eat in in the army, the food was horrible. Murphy couldn't seem to get eggs right unless she boiled them. He recalled the scrambled eggs from Sunday brunch a few weeks earlier—they'd been under-cooked. The sight of slimy egg white floating next to his bacon had al-most undone him. Violet's eyes went wide. She too remembered.

"Oh, you're right," she said. "In that case, I guess you're right, and I'm wrong."

She looked at Ed, her brows still raised, waiting for him to say some-thing. Ed turned his attention back to his plate, eating around the of-fending eggs. Finally, when it was clear that no one would rise to her baiting, Violet did the same.

After putting away the meal—albeit with some effort—they lin-gered a bit longer over coffee. The coffee, they all agreed, was the only thing Murphy did well, extremely well.

Ed looked across the table at Vio-let. An attractive woman, despite her sour disposition; what some would call well preserved. As long as she was occupied with something positive and pleasant, she wasn't too bad to be around. Ed desperately wanted to keep the morning on a positive track.

"Violet," he said. "Last night you were telling us about your Uncle Mortimer. Sounds like an interesting character."

Since the old guy was long since dead, it seemed a safe subject. Violet bit.

"Uncle Mortimer . . . what a pill . . . daddy used to say that Uncle Mortimer was a waste of good air. They were brothers, but they never got along." Her face took on a wistful expression. "He hated everything and everyone. Never had a good word to say about a living soul."

Like someone else we all know, Ed thought, but kept his expression blank.

"He couldn't have been all that bad," Ed said. "After all, he did leave you his entire fortune. He must have liked you."

"I don't think it was so much that he liked me as it was he hated everyone else. And, don't forget, I was the one who found his eyeglasses for him. Everyone else would sit around and giggle behind their hands when he misplaced things. I guess he thought I was salvageable."

Ed had a sense that Violet wasn't telling the whole story of her relationship with her uncle, which was a bit of a problem. He was a man who couldn't resist a puzzle, and her story was just too cryptic—too pat. He had a hard time getting his mind around a man passing all of his relatives by in his will and leaving everything to one who had only found his eyeglasses for him.

"You sure you didn't do other nice things for your uncle . . . things that you've maybe forgotten?"

She scrunched up her forehead and pursed her lips.

"Well . . . let me think . . . no I'm pretty sure that's the only nice thing I ever did for him."

Her eyes darted away when she spoke. Ed knew immediately that she'd lied to him. The question that would nag at him until he found an answer was, why? He'd never known her to lie to him before in all the time they'd known each other. What was it about her uncle that motivated her to seek shelter in lies? He *would* find out. But, he'd have to be discrete—another word for sneaky—and approach the problem indirectly.

"You know, I think you really liked your uncle," he said.

Violet leaned back in her chair, regarding Ed down the length of her nose—a long way to look over her oversized schnozz.

"I am nothing like my uncle," she said with a dose of indignation that had to rate in the high megaton range.

"I didn't say-" Then Ed cut himself off. Violet was a lot of things, but hard of hearing was *not* one of them. He knew very well that she'd heard him clearly. Why had she chosen to respond the way she did? He smiled. This was going to be interesting. "Never mind," he said. "I was just guessing. Can't always be right."

Violet acted like she hadn't heard him. "Well, I suppose I do believe some of the same things he believed. Doesn't make me like him, mind you, because some of his beliefs made perfect sense. For instance, he always used to say, don't try to make omelets if you're not willing to break a few eggs. Now, that makes perfect sense, don't you think."

"I suppose it does." Ed had no idea where that had come from. Rose and Ernesto, who had been silently following the conversation looked like spectators at a tennis match as their heads swiveled from side to side, watching the two gladiators go at it. Ernesto finally broke the mood, by tapping his plate with his fork, causing all eyes to turn to him.

"Hey, amigo," he said. "We have an 8:24 tee time. Don't want to be late."

Golf was one of Ed's passions. He didn't consider himself a good golfer, but he enjoyed testing himself against the course and during a round, he had time to think about other things. He got some of his best ideas while trying to blast out of a greenside bunker—usually unsuccessfully. In fact, the quality of his ideas was often in direct opposition to the quality of his game.

"Okay, compadre, let's get a move on. Our clubs are already at the starter shack." He'd taken them there as soon as he woke up, so they wouldn't have to waste time going back to their homes after brunch.

The path from the community center to the first green of the community's private golf course wound between two six-story condos and transited a street lined on both sides with the little bungalows for those who didn't like apartment living. The houses were small, one-story cottages, in deference to the age of their occupants. No stairs to negotiate. They were identical, with a living room off the main entrance, kitchen and dining room off to the right, and two identically sized bedrooms to the left. Front and back yards were the only means residents had of expressing their individuality. Ed and Ernesto hadn't done anything to the landscaping that was there when they purchased, so their houses were identical, inside and out, and were located across the street from each other. The Wertheim sisters owned a cottage three buildings down from Ed and Ernesto, but had gone hog wild with a profusion of flowers—perennials and annuals—and shrubbery, giving their cottage the appearance of an English country estate, albeit a tiny one.

They arrived at the starter shack at 8:20, to deep frowns from the starter, a rotund man with a Santa Claus beard and a totally bald head named Brian—Ed could never remember his last name. Golfers were asked to arrive 10 minutes prior to tee time. Four minutes was . . . in his words, rude. But, he happened to like Ed and Ernesto, knew they played a fairly fast game, and wouldn't delay foursomes behind them, so he just snorted and gave them their score cards, stubby pencils, and a key to their cart.

The four Koreans who were scheduled to tee off behind them, though, were incensed. They muttered loudly in Korean, glaring at Ed and Ernesto. Ed had nothing against the Korean residents of the community, though he did wonder why they would want to live in such

a place since they hardly ever social-
ized with the non-Korean residents.
Where he found them hard to take,
though, was on the golf course,
where they talked loud, took their
sweet time when you were playing
behind them, but insisted that you
play at warp speed when they were
behind you. He didn't ever recall
seeing one of them smile on the
course. He dealt with them, though,
by ignoring them.

Ernesto on the other hand found
their rude behavior intolerable, and
couldn't resist responding to their
activity.

"Hey, guys," he said. "What's the
problem? You don't want to play behind us or something?"

"You come late," one of the men,
a short, squat man with jet black
hair—from the sheen, from a bottle—and bowlegs. "You should let us
go first."

Ernesto walked over and stood in
front of the man. He had to bend to
be nose to nose.

"Well now, amigo, that ain't gonna happen," he said. "I promise you,
we'll play fast—faster than you
dudes do with your betting and

such. So, just chill your jets."

The man looked confused. He turned and said something in harsh, rapid fire Korean. Ed and Ernesto got in their cart and with Ed driving went to the first tee.

Ernesto leaned out and looked back at the Koreans who were walking behind them, still engaged in an animated conversation.

"Hey, guys," he said. "I better tell you; I'm a postal worker—retired—but, if you keep making that noise behind us, I just might go postal on you."

The four men stopped and stared open mouthed at Ernesto. For all of their pretense of not understanding or speaking good English, they got the significance of 'going postal.'

"You know, Ernesto," Ed said. "One of these days they're gonna call your bluff."

"Well, if they do, I'll just have to go postal, now won't I?" The two men chuckled. "Say, whaddya think about Violet's story about her uncle?"

"What do you mean, what do I think?"

"She got kind of evasive there when you started talking about their relationship."

"You caught that too? I don't know. There's something there she doesn't want to talk about."

"So, you're gonna find out what it is."

It wasn't a question. Ernesto had come to know Ed well, as Ed did him. Ed wasn't surprised that his friend had caught the same vibes he had.

"I'm gonna try," he said. "Now, let's play golf."

They did 'rock, paper, scissors,' to see who would tee off first. Ernesto had scissors, Ed had rock. He laughed.

After hitting his first shot, he stopped laughing. His ball was long, around 280 yards, but was a good ten feet into the long rough on the right.

"You need to work on that slice, amigo," Ernesto said.

"Shut up and hit your ball."

Ernesto went through his pre-shot routine, which involved wiggling his hips and taking several deep breaths. His swing was more

like an attempt to behead the ball
than a golf swing, but he beat Ed's
distance by a good ten yards—in the
left rough.

It went that way for the first eight
holes. On nine, both of them finally
found the fairway, but only by sacri-
ficing more than sixty yards driving
distance. Ed got his first par on
twelve, which he took as a good
omen, because the tee box for thirteen was on a hill overlooking a
small valley containing a small nat-
ural pond that was a favorite stopping place for water fowl. An avid
bird watcher since his teens, Ed
liked to stand on the hill overlooking
the pond to see what species he
could identify.

Because the little dip in the land
was out of play from errant balls
from anywhere on the course, it was
also where Louis Palmer, the
groundskeeper and maintenance
man had constructed his storage
shed. The building's proximity to the
pond, Ed noticed thankfully, didn't
seem to bother the many birds that
congregated on its shores. Nor did
the presence of Palmer, who Ed saw

rolling a gas powered mulcher into the shed.

As they stepped up to the thirteenth tee, Ed let Ernesto and his lengthy pre-shot routine go first, even though his birdie entitled him. While Ernesto did his butt wiggling, Ed walked to the end of the tee box and gazed down at the pond. To his delight, a pair of great blue herons stood in the shallow water at the pond's edge. From the 'awk, awk, awk,' sound they made, and the way they kept clacking their beaks together, he figured them for a nesting pair. Just as he turned to prepare to take his shot, a flock of Canada geese swooped in, honking loudly as they splashed into the middle of the pond. The herons continued to make their courting sounds, ignoring the raucous geese. Ed smiled broadly. *Nice how nature lets creatures coexist.*

On thirteen he hit the ball down the middle of the fairway a scorching two hundred ninety yards, made the green in two and one-putted. *Who said thirteen was an unlucky number?*

THREE

Golf ended as it usually did; Ernesto was ahead so many strokes by hole thirteen that Ed decided to quit keeping score. On their way back to the clubhouse to turn in the cart, they noticed the Korean foursome just teeing off on ten. Ernesto could resist waving at them. They refused to look back.

"Hey, leave 'em alone," Ed said.

Ernesto shrugged. "Sorry, I can't help it. They're so self- righteous, and never, I mean never, admit when they make a mistake."

"Yeah, well, you shouldn't let it get to you. What do you want to do for lunch?"

Violet and Rose invited us to a late lunch at their place, don't you remember?"

After parking their cart, they took their clubs for the trek along the path between the condos to Wisteria Lane. They took both sets of clubs to Ed's house.

They had a standing bet; loser cleaned the winner's clubs; and even though they'd stopped keeping score, Ed conceded that Ernesto would have won. In fact, in their years of playing together, Ed had only twice *not* been the one to clean the clubs.

"Okay, I'm taking a shower and changing," Ed said after they stacked the clubs against the wall on the patio. "I'll come over in about thirty minutes and we can walk down to Rose and Violet's place."

After Ernesto left, Ed went to his garage, where he kept his old silver Toyota 4-Runner, and got a bucket, a scrub brush and an old bathroom towel from a rack beneath the tool bench. He filled the bucket from the faucet at the back of his house and began scrubbing the clubs, starting with the irons. After removing dirt and grass particles from the club faces and hozzles, he rubbed them dry with the towel. He then repeated the same process with the woods, taking particular care with the drivers.

The clubs were stacked in two groups, in order from driver to putter, next to the golf bags. Leaving them to dry in the sun, he carefully wiped off his golf shoes and draped the towel over the back of a wicker chair, and then, after dumping the dirty water around the roots of the azalea bush at the corner of his patio, took the bucket and brush back to the garage.

He went inside and to the bathroom where he removed his golf shoes and clothing, at first dumping everything on the floor in an untidy pile, but as he dumped his underwear, he heard his late wife's voice in his mind. *Edward Lazenby, don't you be leaving your dirty clothes piled on the floor like that. That's what we have laundry hampers for.* He felt a burning in his eyes, unshed tears, even as he smiled. Victoria had been like that—a place for everything, and everything in its place. He chuckled. She always nagged him about tidiness, which annoyed him at the time, but he really missed it now that she was gone. The memories came back at the oddest times and places, and even after five years, he still missed her. Sometimes, he resented the fact that ovarian cancer had stolen her chance to enjoy retirement with him.

He shook it off. *The past is something that can't be undone.* Something else she'd often say whenever he bemoaned some missed opportunity. He turned on the water, as hot as he could stand, and stood underneath the shower, letting the hot water cascade over him.

Shower finished, he toweled off, shaved, and brushed his hair until it had just the right amount of wave. He then dressed in a pair of tan slacks and a powder blue polo shirt, topping that off with tan socks and a pair of brown leather loafers, buffed to a mirror-like shine. He checked the time as he slipped his Bulova watch onto his right wrist— fifteen minutes until the lunch with the Wertheim sisters.

He walked across the street to Ernesto's house. His friend opened the door just as he was reaching for the buzzer.

"Hey, bro," Ernesto said. "You clean up nice."

The one thing Ed could always count on was Ernesto ribbing him about the way he dressed. He stood there in his doorway, wearing a pair of khaki cargo pants that ended mid-calf, with a puke green long sleeved shirt that looked as if it had been taken directly from the dryer with no ironing to remove the wrinkles, outside the pants. Sockless, on his size twelve feet he had pink flip flops. It was warm for October, so light dress was appropriate, but Ernesto looked like he had just returned from a scavenger hunt through the Montgomery County landfill.

"Ernie, my boy," Ed said. "I wish I could say the same for you."

Ernesto looked down at his feet. He lifted the edge of his shirt with his pudgy fingers.

"What's wrong with what I'm wearing?"

"Nothing if you're going dumpster diving."

"Hey, it's just lunch with Violet and Rose, man. It's not like we're going to some fancy afternoon tea."

Ed knew, though, that with the Wertheim's, especially Violet, it *was* likely to be just that. Even though they'd been born and raised in

Rockville, Maryland, and had never been south of Richmond, Virginia in their lives, she had what amounted to an obsession with the plantation society of the antebellum south. She was likely to be wearing a dress with plenty of wide petticoats and a scooped neckline. Rose, accustomed to living in her older sister's shadow, would be similarly dressed. If the two of them had been the fussy type, he would be considered un-derdressed, but thankfully, Rose never fussed about anything, and Violet never paid much attention to what other people wore, so they would accept him. Ernesto they would also accept, because he was . . . Ernesto. Even though he was al-ways threatening to 'go postal,' he was such an outgoing, friendly, bear of a man, everyone liked him. Ed suspected that Rose actually had something of a romantic thing for him.

"Well, if you feel comfortable, I guess that's the only thing that mat-ters," he said. "We still have almost fifteen minutes, and you know Violet and Rose never start anything on time. It's only a three minute walk to their house, so what'll we do to kill time."

"I think I hear a hint in there somewhere. You wouldn't be suggesting a little before lunch sip, would you, maybe a touch of bourbon on the rocks?"

"Why, Ernesto Cardozo, I do believe you're a mind reader."

"Nah, just an old postman who learned to know what people wanted . . . come on in."

He stepped aside and let Ed enter, then followed him into the living room. Ed flopped down on the sofa while Ernesto poured two fingers of amber liquid from a square bottle with a black label into two water glasses.

"Jim Bcam Black," Ed said. "You're moving up in the world."

"You gonna drink, drink the best. None of that rotgut passing itself off as whiskey for me."

Ed chuckled as he took a sip. It was good whiskey. *If he only had the same taste in clothes.* But, hey, it didn't matter. Friends didn't obsess over such trivialities as clothing—especially friends who were getting as long in the tooth as the two of them were. It wasn't as if either of them had to dress to impress the ladies any longer. He looked at his watch.

"Shouldn't we be going?"

Ernesto drained the last of his drink and reached for the bottle.

"Hell, we have time for one more . . . don't you think?"

Ed looked at his glass. He had about a finger of liquor left. *Damn, I didn't even notice drinking it. It is smooth, though. Oh, what the hell.* He drained the glass and held it out to allow Ernesto to pour in another two fingers.

"You want ice?" Ernesto asked.

Ed sniffed. The woody odor warmed his nose.

"No, I'll just do this one neat." He took a sip and sighed.

"Yeah, no point spoiling good bourbon with ice," Ernesto agreed and took a sip as well.

They finished the second drinks in companionable silence. After draining his glass, Ed put his glass on the coffee table, which was covered with rings from previous drinking sessions.

"Well, I think we should get go-ing," he said. "We'll be fashionably late; I don't want to be sloshed along with it."

Ernesto frowned. He looked long-ingly at his glass. Then, he sighed and drained it, and placed it next to Ed's on the table.

"Yeah, I guess you're right."

He teetered slightly as he stood, but after taking a deep breath, steadied himself.

By the time they were outside, and Ernesto was locking his door, he was rock steady. Ed marveled at the man's ability to metabolize alco-hol. He was still a bit unsteady him-self, and was sure Violet would give them grief as soon as she smelled the booze on their breath. He cursed himself for forgetting to put breath mints in his pocket, and then shrugged. He remembered the old joke he'd heard in the army, 'what do you get when you spray air freshener in an elevator after some-one farts? The smell of a fart in a pine forest.' The mints would only add itself to the whiskey smell. He would just have to endure Violet's nagging.

The brisk air helped clear his head, so that by the time they arrived at the Wertheim's house, the effects of the whiskey on Ed had mostly worn off. He rang the bell. When the door swung inward, he turned his head to minimize the possibility of his whiskey breath giving him away too soon.

Rose Wertheim, wearing a yellow frock that stopped just below her knees, stood in the door. Instead of her usual smile, she wore a worried look. She stepped aside and allowed Ed and Ernesto to enter the living room. As he passed her, Ed noticed that she didn't make eye contact. In fact, she hadn't greeted them as she usually did.

"Rose," he asked. "Is something wrong?"

Her eyes darted to her left.

"Uh, well . . . I . . . why don't you two come on in and have a seat."

When Ed followed her gaze, he saw that there was another person present, and that it wasn't her sister Violet. It took Ed a few seconds to recognize Peony Lake, the only daughter of Violet and Rose's younger sister, Daisy. Daisy, Ed had been told, had died in an auto accident when Peony was thirteen, and she'd lived with her two aunts until she graduated high school and went off to college. Now thirty, she worked as a graphics designer in New York, and only came to visit her aunts on holidays. Unlike her aunts, though, she was not into formal dress. If anything, with her faded blue jeans, cut outs showing her bony knees, and a wrinkled New York Mets sweatshirt, she looked more like Ernesto's relative or drinking buddy, than a Wertheim. Her dark brown hair was cropped close to her narrow skull. She sat on the couch, clutching a glass of red wine in her right hand and a wrinkled sheet of paper in her left.

Warning signals went off in Ed's head. Rose's nervousness and Peony's presence—and, Violet's absence—something was wrong.

He turned on Rose. "Okay, Rose, I know something's wrong. Where's Violet? What's going on?"

Peony put her wineglass down and stood.

"Hello, Mr. Lazenby," she said as she walked toward him. "It's been a while." She extended a slender hand.

Ed shook her hand. Her grip was firm and dry. "Hi, Peony, nice to see you, too, although I didn't expect you to visit until Thanksgiving."

"Uh, yeah. I came down to visit Aunt Rose and Aunt Vi to discuss a personal problem I'm having."

Ernesto came up behind Ed.

"Having man problems, Peony?" he asked.

Her cheeks flamed red, and she glared at him.

"Cut the kid some slack, Ernesto," Ed said to defuse the tension. "Besides, there's something else wrong. I can feel it. right, ladies?"

Peony laughed. "I see Aunt Vi was right about you."

"Right about me what?" Ed's left brow rose.

"She said you were very perceptive; that nothing got past you. You're right, there is another problem, one we need your help on."

"What kind of problem?"

"Aunt Violet's been kidnapped," she said. She handed him the paper.

FOUR

After handing Ed the paper, Peony put her arms around her aunt's shoulder and led her to the couch where they both sat; Rose looking confused and Peony looking stone faced. Ed couldn't help notice that, sitting so close together, the two women looked more like sisters than Rose and Violet looked when they were together. He then looked down at the paper Peony had handed him.

It was a simple sheet of 8 by 10-inch bond paper—the kind you can buy by the ream in any CVS or Office Depot—covered with letters and words that, from the glossy paper, had been cut from magazines. The fragments had been glued to the paper in precise lines, centered on the sheet.

WE HAVE TAKEN VIOLET
DO NOT CALL THE POLICE
OR WE WILL KILL HER
WE WILL CONTACT YOU
LATER WITH OUR DEMANDS

"Holy shit," Ernesto said. He'd been peering over Ed's shoulder. "We gotta call the cops."

"No!" Rose and Peony spoke as one. Peony rose from the sofa.

"You read it. If we call the police, they'll kill her," she said.

Ed shook his head. He ran a hand over his head.

"She's right, Ernesto," he said. "We can't take a chance like that with Violet's life."

"Okay, okay, I guess you're right, but what are we gonna do?"

Ed looked over at the two women.

"First, I want you two to tell us what happened. Who gave you the note?"

Rose and Peony looked at each other. The younger woman then looked at Ed. "It was on the coffee table when Aunt Rose and I got back from the grocery store," she said, clearly taking charge.

"So, Violet was here alone," Ed said. "How long?"

"Oh, I don't know . . . thirty minutes, maybe an hour. Do you remember, Aunt Rose?"

Rose shook her head. She kept

her gaze focused on the coffee table.

"I-I . . . I suppose so . . . an hour sounds . . . right."

"And when we got back, we came from the garage to the kitchen through the back door," Peony said. "We called to let Aunt Vi know we were back, and received no answer, so we looked for her in the bedroom, but she wasn't there either."

Ed looked around the room. He tried to picture in his head the two women entering the kitchen and calling out for Violet.

"What did you do then?"

"We came in here. Aunt Rose noticed the paper on the coffee table. That's it."

"When did all this happen?" Ed asked.

"I don't know, maybe twenty minutes ago . . . or less," she said. "Just before the two of you came."

"Who do you think is doing this?" Ernesto asked.

Rose shook her head again. "I don't know," she said. "We don't know hardly any people outside the community except Peony. She's just about the only relative we have left."

"What are we going to do?" Peony asked, looking directly at Ed.

Ed sighed. Responsibility for managing this mess was being thrust upon him, a responsibility he didn't want, but he saw no way to avoid it.

"For now, there's not much we can do but wait," he said. "We'll see what the kidnapper's next demands are, and then decide. In the meantime, I want you to walk me through the morning in as much detail as you can; everything you remember."

"Why?" Rose asked in a querulous voice. "How will that help get Violet back?"

"I don't know, but the more information I have the better I'll be able to come up with some kind of plan. Besides, sometimes it's the seemingly insignificant details that can be the most important, so humor me."

"He's probably right, Aunt Rose," Peony said. Ed felt grateful for her rational response.

"So, maybe Ernesto and I can take you two ladies out for lunch," he said. "There's a Pizza place down on Georgia Avenue. We can talk while we eat."

"We were planning to eat here," Rose said. "I made a nice Caesar salad and tuna sandwiches."

"Sure, if that's what you want," Ed said. "I just figured you'd rather not be bothered with cooking. I suppose it is a better idea, though. We need to be here for the kidnapper's next note."

He was still having trouble getting his mind around the idea of someone kidnapping Violet Wertheim. Other than her comments about her uncle leaving her his estate, he'd never heard either sister mention any degree of wealth before. They tended toward the eccentric in their dress, but drove a tcn-ycar-old Buick, and had no more, or more expensive looking, jewelry than any of the other ladies in PVC. Neither of them went outside the community very often, other than the occasional trip to Washington to attend concerts at Kennedy Center, and Ed doubted that they rated any kind of news coverage—but, he made a mental note to check that. It made no sense, yet he held the note in his hand. It looked like the real deal.

Ed and Ernesto sat at the dining table while Rose and Peony brought food in from the kitchen. The men offered to help, but were told to sit and pour themselves iced tea. The two women returned, each carrying a platter, one with a stack of toasted tuna sandwiches, the other with a bowl of Caesar salad.

Peony sat at the foot of the small dining table, nearest the kitchen, with Rose opposite her. Ed sat to Peony's left, with Ernesto opposite him. Peony passed the platter of sandwiches to Ed and the salad to Ernesto. The two containers of food arrived in front of Rose at the same time, causing her to pause in confusion while she looked as if she was undecided about which to take first.

When rose noticed that everyone was watching her, she blushed.

"Oh, I'm sorry," she said. "I was thinking of Violet. I guess my mind wandered."

She took a sandwich, and then put a large helping of salad onto the plate next to it.

Ed let everyone eat a few bites

before beginning his quizzing of the two women. He didn't take notes. During his twenty five years working as a systems analyst at the Defense Department he'd learned to retain essential information in his memory rather than having to take written notes. His handwriting was so crabby his notes were often indecipherable anyway. By the time they'd finished the salad and sandwiches and were in the living room with glasses of cabernet sauvignon, Ed had gleaned the following scenario from Rose and Peony:

10:30 pm Friday night – Peony had arrived at National Airport from New York City. It took her time to retrieve her bags and get a taxi to bring her to PVC, located on Norbeck Road, four miles north of Georgia Avenue in Montgomery County.

1:15 am Saturday – Peony arrived at the Wertheim home.

7:15 am – Violet and Rose have lunch with Ed and Ernesto at the community center.

8:15 am – Violet and Rose return

home.

11:40 am – Rose and Peony go shopping.

12:15 – 12:20 – Rose and Peony return home to find kidnap note.

Ed ran the list of actions through his mind, looking for inconsistencies or relationships. Nothing immediately stood out. No red flags gave him pause. But, his lizard brain itched like crazy, because *something*, what it was he had no idea, just wasn't right. He just couldn't put his finger on it.

Until they heard from the kidnapper, though, there didn't seem to be much he could do. He sat and fidgeted. Then, it occurred to him that he was sitting in the middle of a crime scene, a crime scene that no one had examined.

"Okay, listen up everyone," Ed said. "I want you all to sit right where you are. I'm gonna take a look around and see if there are any clues the kidnapper might have left when he took Violet."

The two women gave him puzzled looks, but Ernesto only nodded.

He started with the living room,

checking from the entrance doorway and then around from left to right, looking for anything out of place. There were no indications of any kind of struggle. The windows were all closed and locked, none of the furniture looked to have been moved from where he remembered seeing it the last time he was there, and the four little wooden hampers containing several years' worth of gardening magazines still sat in the corner of the room near the sofa.

"Were the doors locked when you came back from the store?" he asked over his shoulder.

"Yes, both front and back doors were locked. The front still had the security chain in place," Rose responded.

He rubbed his chin, looked around once more and moved on to the dining room. Nothing out of place there—same for the kitchen. He checked the door carefully to see if there'd been any attempts to get at the lock—nothing. The kitchen itself was as neat as a pin. A spatula and spoon in the sink were the only things out of place. The trash bin

Charles Ray

was empty and looked like it had
been washed, something that the
sisters did much to the amusement
of their neighbors, but Rose always
insisted that cleanliness was next to
godliness.

He went back to the living room.

"Rose, you mind if I check the
bedrooms?"

"Uh, I don't know, Ed," she said.
"I mean, a man going into a lady's
boudoir-"

"Oh, Aunt Rose," Peony said.
"Don't be such a prude. He's just investigating."

"We-l-l-l, I suppose so, but you
stay out of my unmentionables, Edward Lazenby."

He checked both bedrooms and
their adjoining bathrooms, avoiding
the drawers, and saw the same as
he'd seen in the rest of the house—a
whole lot of nothing.

Back in the living room, he sat
on the chair at the right of the sofa
and put his hands on his knees.

"Not much we can do now," he
said. "But, sit and wait."

Other books by this author:

Al Pennyback mysteries

Color Me Dead
Memorial to the Dead
Deadline
Dead, White, and Blue
A Good Day to Die
The Day the Music Died
Die, Sinner
Deadly Intentions
Death by Design
Till Death Do Us Part
Deadly Dose
Dead Man's Cove
Dead Men Don't Answer
Deadly Paradise
Kiss of Death
Death in White Satin
Death and Taxis
Deadbeat
A Deadly Wind Blows
Death Wish
Deadly Vendetta
A Time to Kill, A Time to Die
Dead Ringer

Charles Ray

Ed Lazenby mysteries
Butterfly Effect
Coriolis Effect

The Buffalo Soldier series:

Buffalo Soldier: Trial by Fire
Buffalo Soldier: Homecoming
Buffalo Soldier: Incident at Cactus Junction
Buffalo Soldier: Peacekeepers
Buffalo Soldier: Renegade
Buffalo Soldier: Escort Duty
Buffalo Soldier: Battle at Dead Man's Gulch
Buffalo Soldier: Yosemite
Buffalo Soldier: Comanchero
Buffalo Soldier: Range War
Buffalo Soldier: Mob Justice
Buffalo Soldier: Chasing Ghosts

Other fiction
Angel on His Shoulder
She's No Angel
Child of the Flame
Pip's Revenge
Here, There Be Demons
Wallace in Underland
Further Adventures of Wallace in Underland

Dead Letter and Other Tales
The White Dragons
The Dragon's Lair
Dragon Slayer
The Last Gunfighters
The Culling
*Frontier Justice: Bass Reeves, Depu-
ty*
  U.S. Marshal
*Angel on His Shoulder-Revised Edi-
tion*
Battle at the Galactic Junkyard
Mountain Man
Devil's Lake

Nonfiction

*Things I Learned from My Grand-
mother About*
  Leadership and Life
*Taking Charge: Effective Leadership
for the*
  Twenty-first Century
Grab the Brass ring
*African Places: A Photographic Jour-
ney*
  *Through Zimbabwe and southern
Africa*
A Portrait of Africa
There's Always a Plan B

*In the Line of Fire: American Diplo-
mats in
  the Trenches
Advice for the Insecure Writer
Looking at Life Through My Lens*

Children's books
*The Yak and the Yeti
Samantha and the Bully
Molly Learns to Share
Where is Teddy?
Catie and Mister Hop-Hop*

See these and other books by this
author   at:
http://www.amazon.com/Charles-
Ray/e/B006WMLEZK

About the Author

Charles Ray has been writing fiction since his teens. He won a Sunday school magazine writing contest when he was thirteen, and having his byline on a short story published in a national publication forever hooked him on writing. During his time in the army (1962-1982) he often moonlighted as a newspaper or magazine journalist, and was the editorial cartoonist for the Spring Lake (NC) News, a weekly newspaper, during the 1970s. In addition to his writing, he was an artist/cartoonist and photographer for a number of publications, including Ebony, Eagle and Swan, and Essence, and had a monthly cartoon feature and did several covers for Buffalo, a now-defunct magazine that was dedicated to showcasing the contributions of African-

Charles Ray

Americans to the country's military history.

After retiring from the army, he joined the U.S. Foreign Service, and served as a diplomat in posts in Asia and Africa until his retirement in 2012. He has worked and traveled throughout the world (Antarctica is the only continent he hasn't visited), and now, as a full time writer, continues to globetrot looking for interesting things to write about, draw, or take pictures of.

A native of Texas, he now calls Maryland home. For more on his writing and other projects, check one of the following Web sites:

http://charlesaray.blogspot.com
http://charlieray45.wordpress.com
http://www.twitter.com/charlieray45
http://www.facebook.com/charlieray45
http://www.flickr.com/photos/charlesray45/
http://www.viewbug.com/member/charlesray

Photo by Denise Ray-Wickersham

Charles Ray

www.ingramcontent.com/pod-product-compliance
Lightning Source LLC
Chambersburg PA
CBHW071454170626
46811CB00007B/2575